MARVEL

MARVEL ACTION

AVENGERS

THE LIVING NIGHTMARE

Marvel Publishing:

VP Production & Special Projects: Jeff Youngquist
Editor, Juvenile Publishing: Lauren Bisom
Assistant Editor, Special Projects: Caitlin O'Connell
VP, Licensed Publishing: Sven Larsen
SVP Print, Sales & Marketing: David Gabriel
Editor In Chief: C.B. Cebulski

IDW Publishing:

Collection Edits
ALONZO SIMON
and ZAC BOONE

Original Collection Design
CHRISTA MIESNER

Production Artist
VALERIA LOPEZ

Cover Artist
JON SOMMARIVA

Jerry Bennington, President

Nachie Marsham, Publisher

Cara Morrison, Chief Financial Officer

Matthew Ruzicka, Chief Accounting Officer

Rebekah Cahalin, EVP of Operations

John Barber, Editor-in-Chief

Justin Eisinger, Editorial Director, Graphic Novels and Collections

Scott Dunbier, Director, Special Projects

Blake Kobashigawa, VP of Sales

Anna Morrow, Sr Marketing Director

Tara McCrillis, Director of Design & Production

Mike Ford, Director of Operations

Shauna Monteforte, Sr. Director of Manufacturing Operations

Ted Adams and Robbie Robbins, IDW Founders

ISBN: 978-1-68405-636-1   24 23 22 21   1 2 3 4

Special thanks: **Tom Brevoort**

Originally published as MARVEL ACTION: AVENGERS issues #10–12.

For international rights, contact licensing@idwpublishing.com

MARVEL
MARVEL ACTION
AVENGERS
THE LIVING NIGHTMARE

WRITTEN BY **MATTHEW K. MANNING**

ART BY **MARCIO FIORITO**

ADDITIONAL ART BY **NUNO PLATI**

COLORS BY **PROTOBUNKER**

LETTERS BY **CHRISTA MIESNER**

ASSISTANT EDITS BY **MEGAN BROWN**

EDITED BY **BOBBY CURNOW**

AVENGERS CREATED BY
STAN LEE & JACK KIRBY

ART BY: JON SOMMARIVA

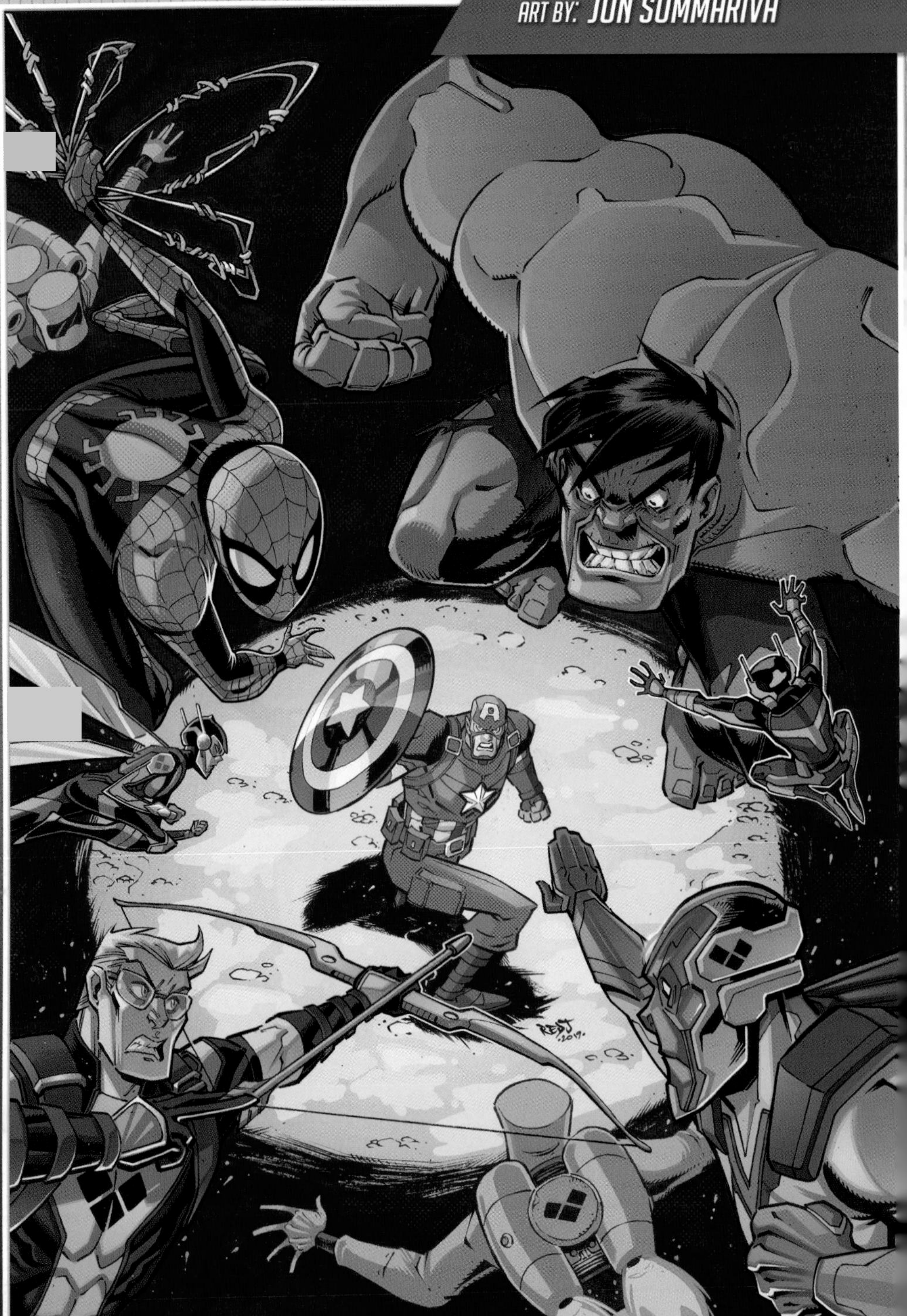

CAPTAIN AMERICA NO LONGER REMEMBERS THE SECOND WORLD WAR.

HE DOESN'T REMEMBER CIVILIAN LIFE AS A YOUNG MAN NAMED STEVE ROGERS.

HE DOESN'T REMEMBER THE SERUM THAT TURNED HIM INTO A SUPER HERO.

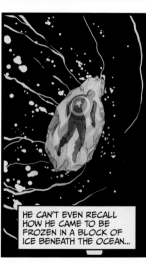

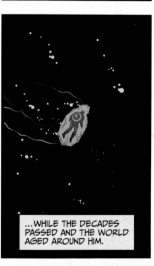

INTO AN AMERICAN ICON.

HE CAN'T EVEN RECALL HOW HE CAME TO BE FROZEN IN A BLOCK OF ICE BENEATH THE OCEAN...

...WHILE THE DECADES PASSED AND THE WORLD AGED AROUND HIM.

BUT MOST IMPORTANT, EVEN THOUGH HE KNOWS THAT THE AVENGERS FOUND HIM YEARS AGO AND RESCUED HIM FROM THE ICE...

...CAPTAIN AMERICA CAN NO LONGER REMEMBER...

...WAKING UP.

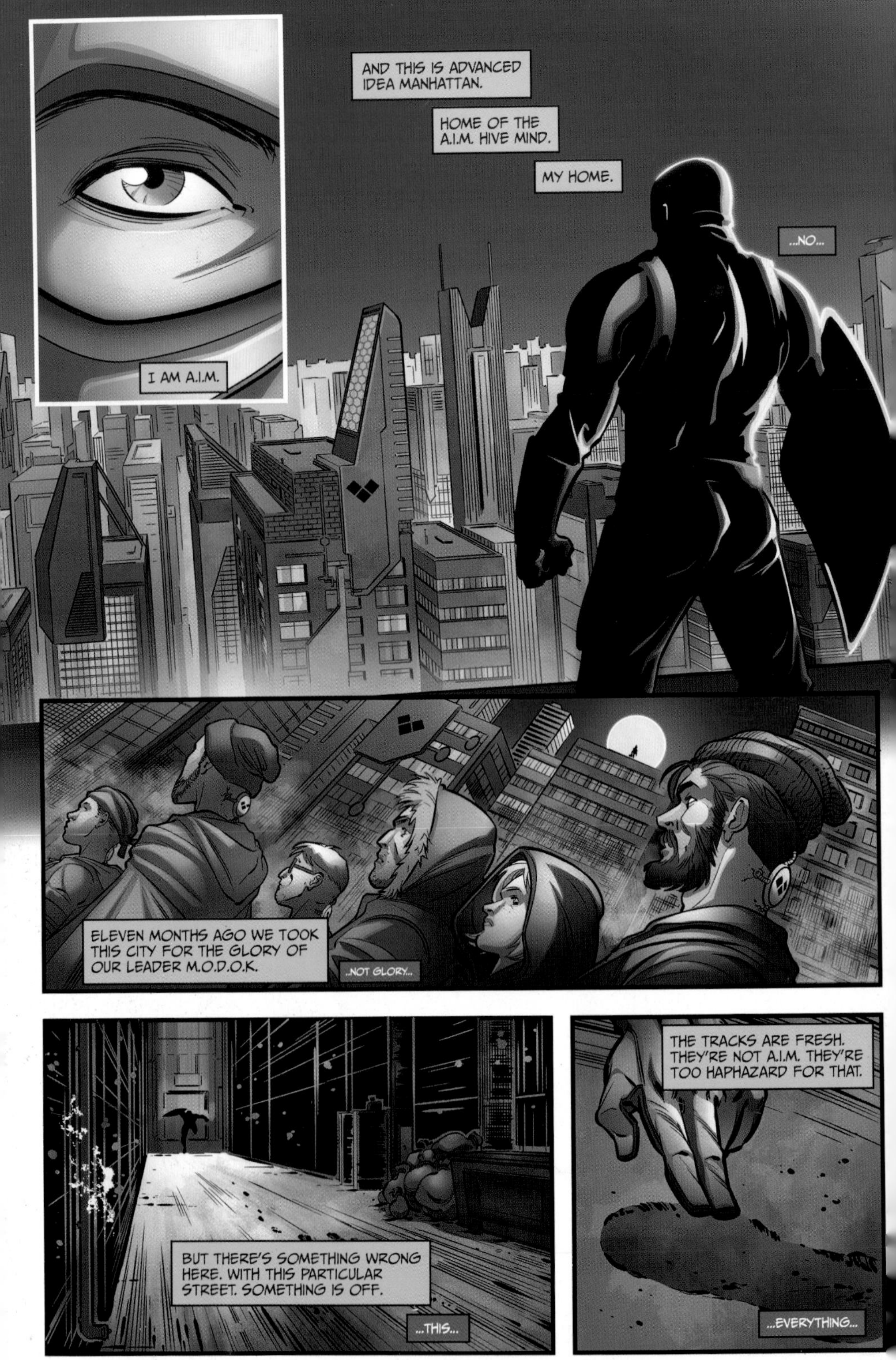
I AM A.I.M.
AND THIS IS ADVANCED IDEA MANHATTAN.
HOME OF THE A.I.M. HIVE MIND.
MY HOME.
...NO...
ELEVEN MONTHS AGO WE TOOK THIS CITY FOR THE GLORY OF OUR LEADER M.O.D.O.K.
..NOT GLORY...
BUT THERE'S SOMETHING WRONG HERE. WITH THIS PARTICULAR STREET. SOMETHING IS OFF.
...THIS...
THE TRACKS ARE FRESH. THEY'RE NOT A.I.M. THEY'RE TOO HAPHAZARD FOR THAT.
...EVERYTHING...

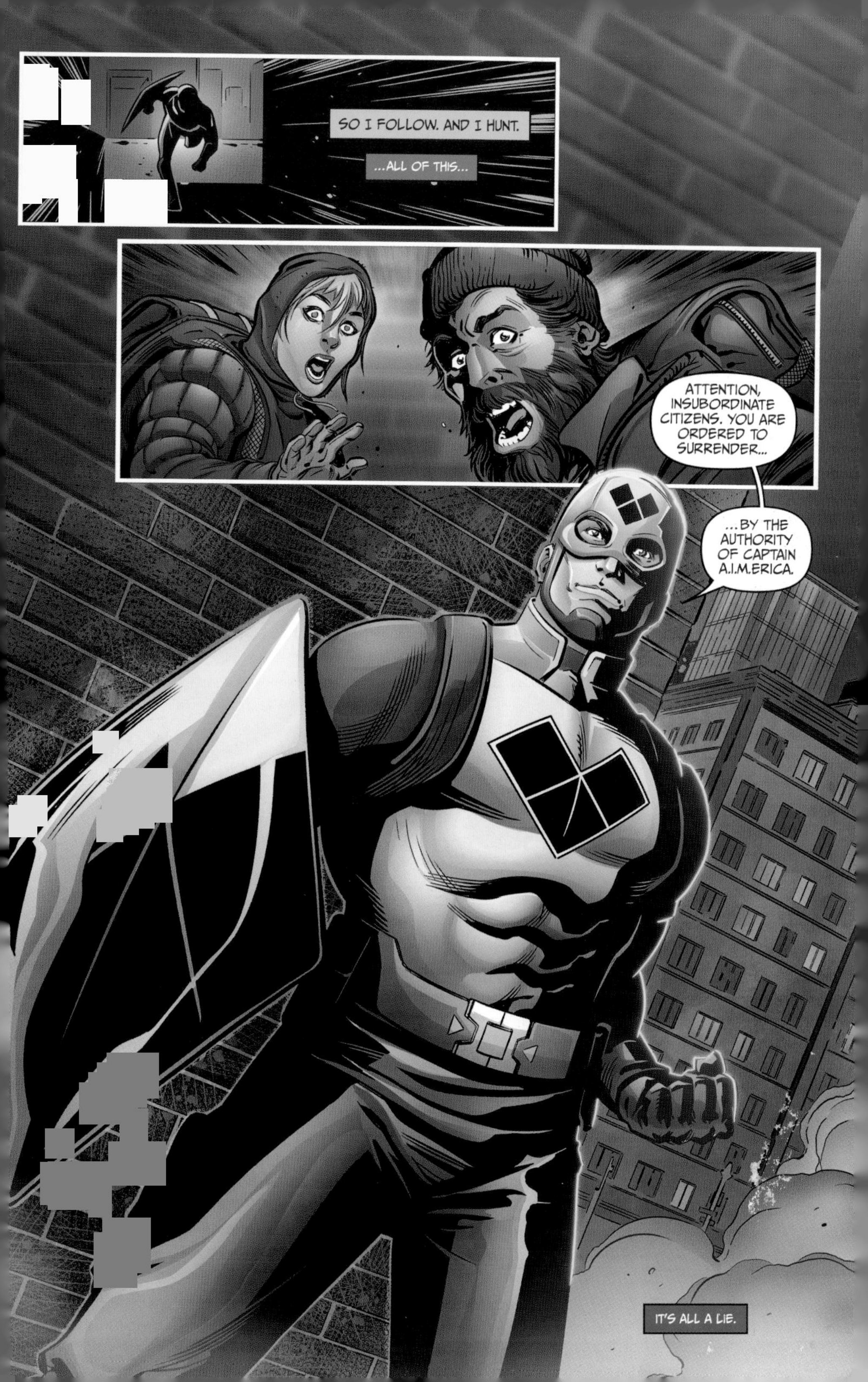
SO I FOLLOW. AND I HUNT.
...ALL OF THIS...
ATTENTION, INSUBORDINATE CITIZENS. YOU ARE ORDERED TO SURRENDER...
...BY THE AUTHORITY OF CAPTAIN A.I.M.ERICA.
IT'S ALL A LIE.

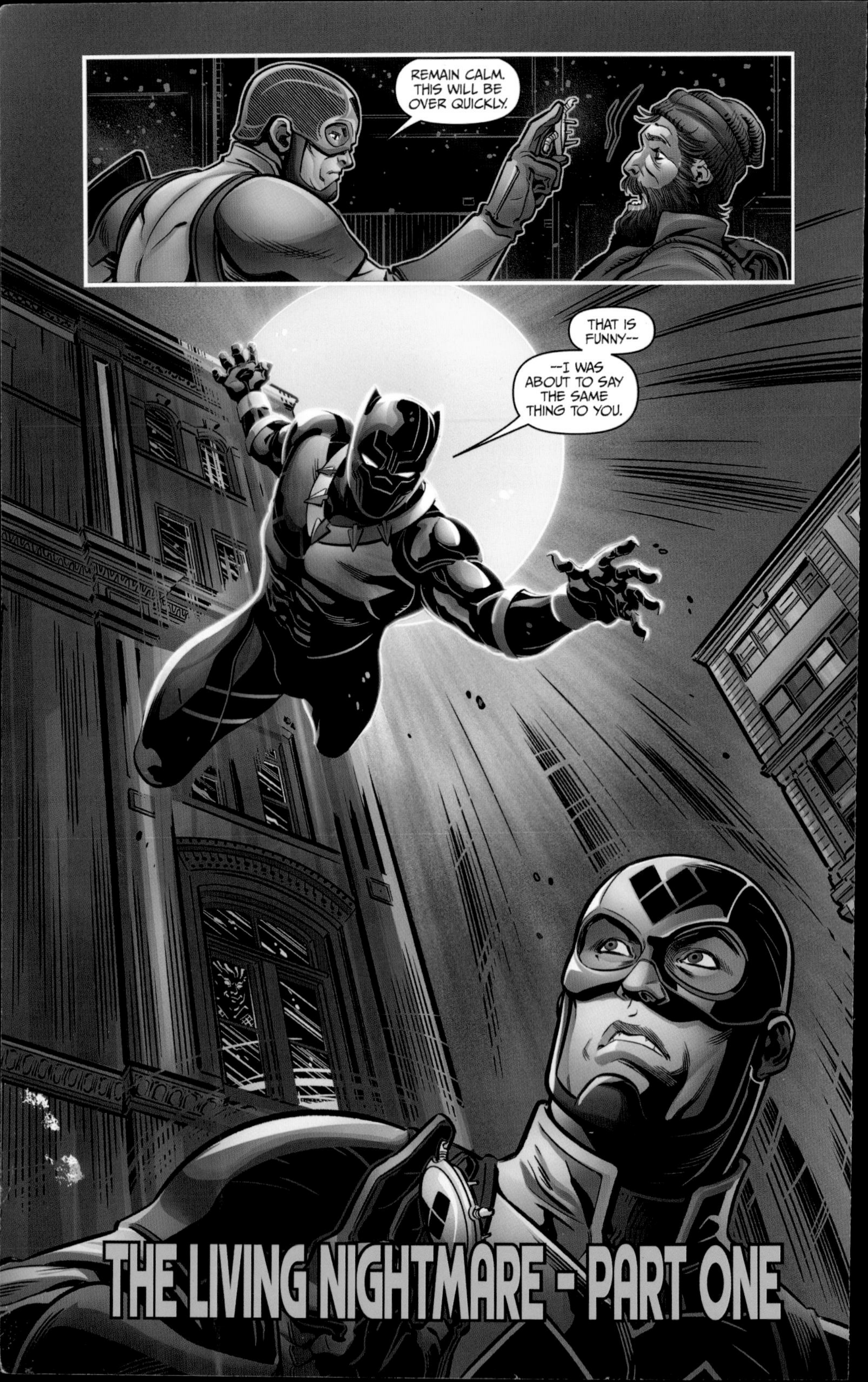
REMAIN CALM. THIS WILL BE OVER QUICKLY.
THAT IS FUNNY--
--I WAS ABOUT TO SAY THE SAME THING TO YOU.
THE LIVING NIGHTMARE - PART ONE

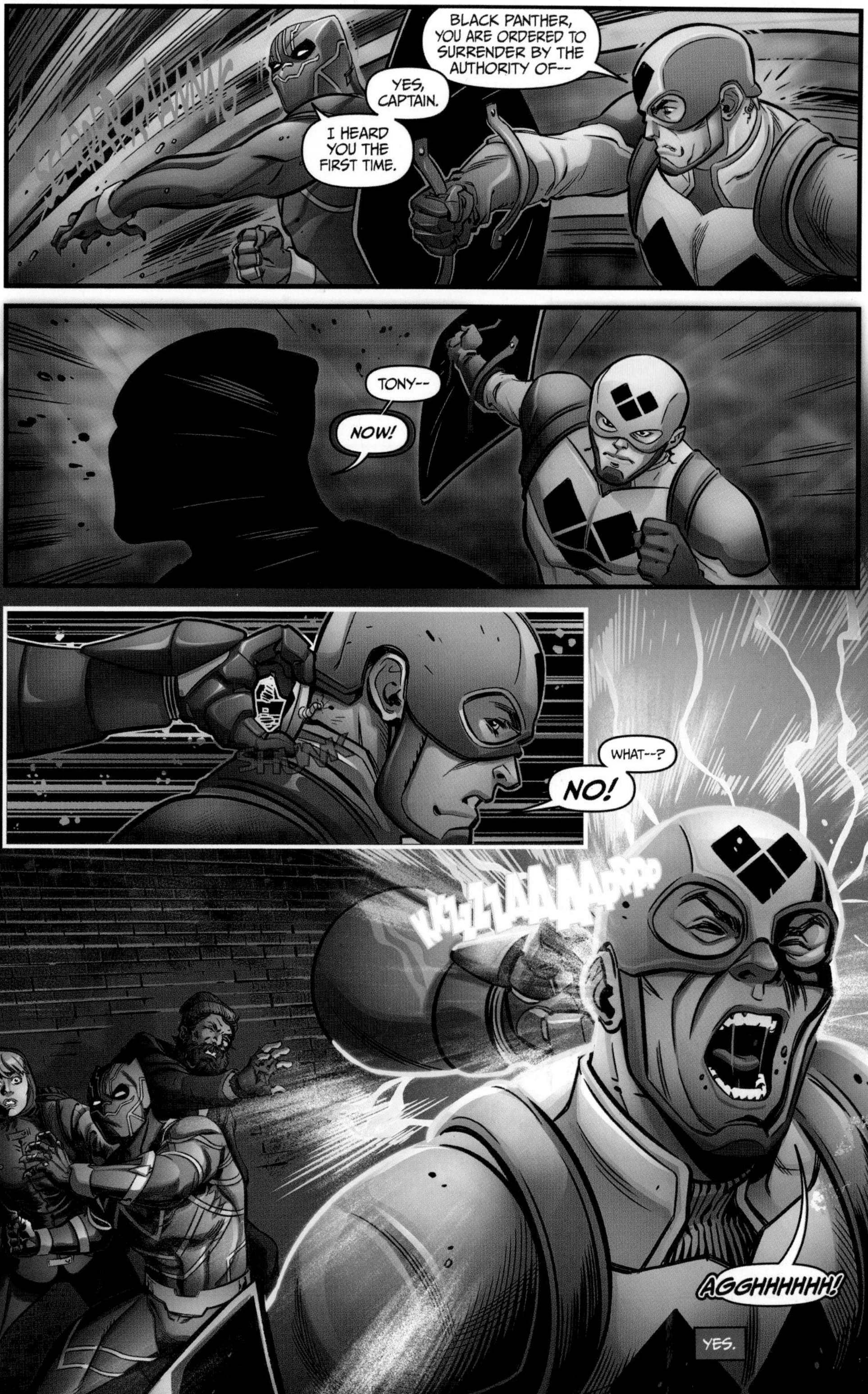
BLACK PANTHER, YOU ARE ORDERED TO SURRENDER BY THE AUTHORITY OF--
YES, CAPTAIN.
I HEARD YOU THE FIRST TIME.
TONY--
NOW!
WHAT--?
NO!
AGGHHHHHH!
YES.

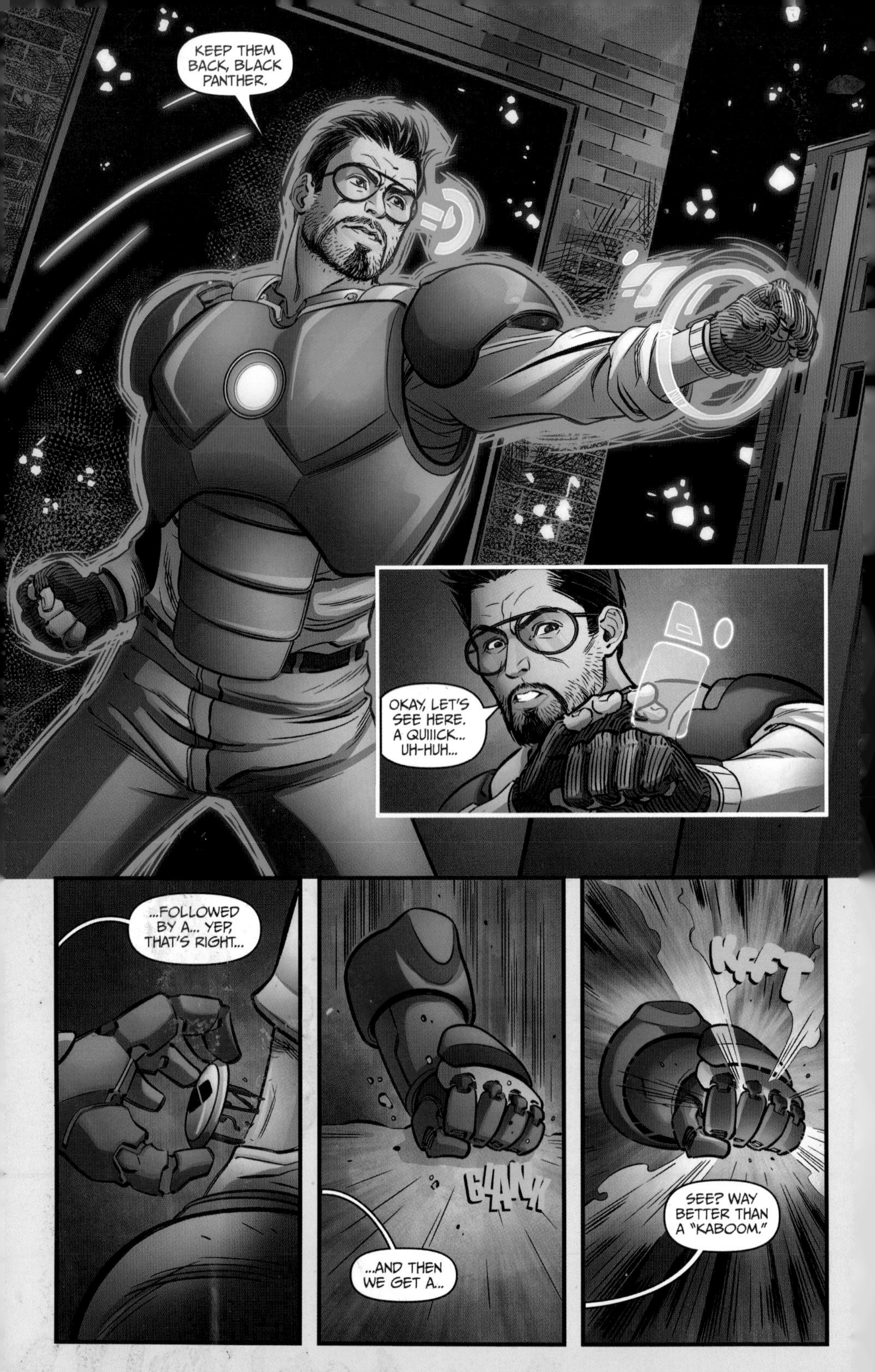
KEEP THEM BACK, BLACK PANTHER.
OKAY, LET'S SEE HERE. A QUIIICK... UH-HUH...
...FOLLOWED BY A... YEP, THAT'S RIGHT...
...AND THEN WE GET A...
KRFT
SEE? WAY BETTER THAN A "KABOOM."

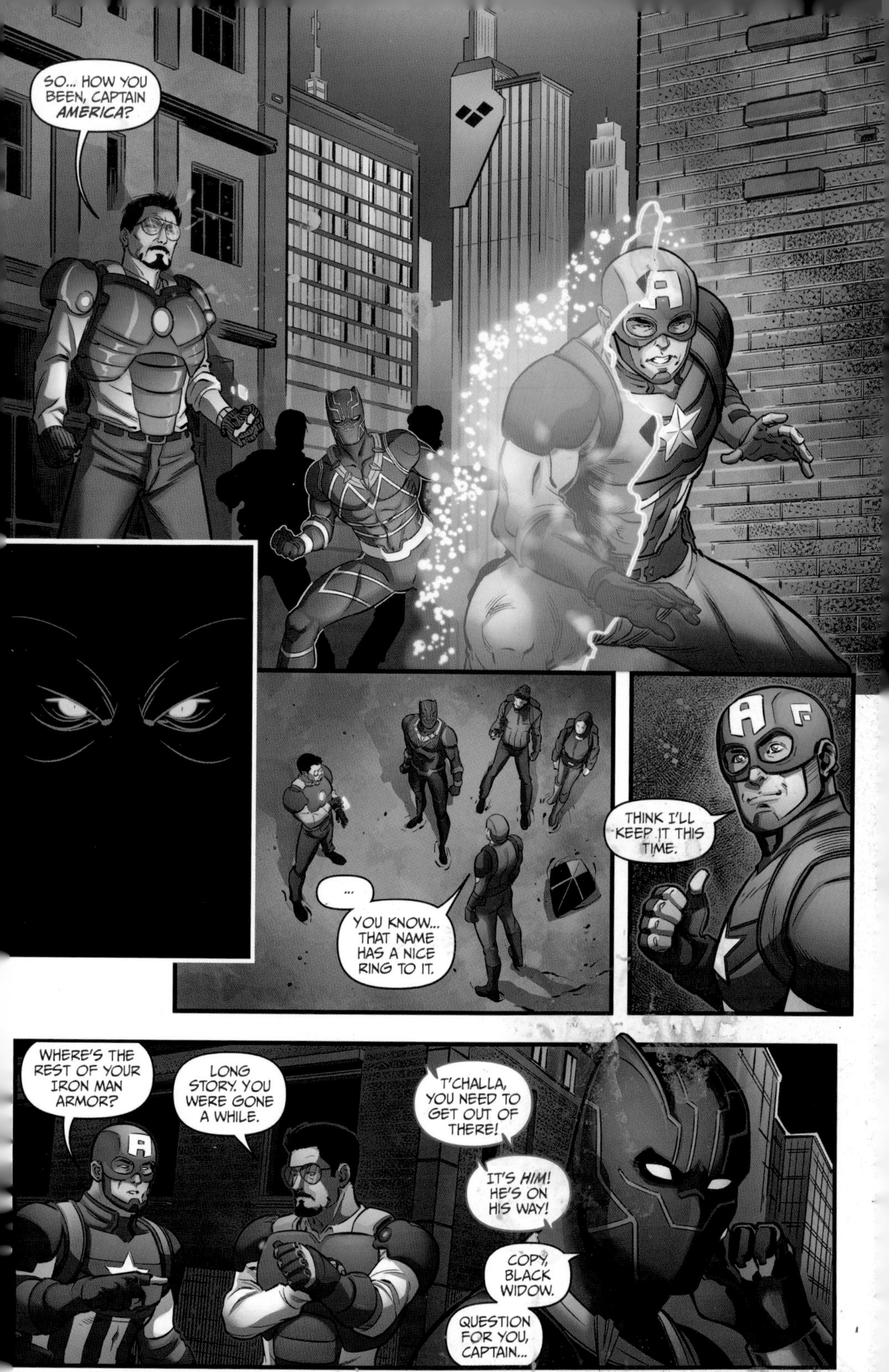
SO... HOW YOU BEEN, CAPTAIN AMERICA?
...
YOU KNOW... THAT NAME HAS A NICE RING TO IT.
THINK I'LL KEEP IT THIS TIME.
WHERE'S THE REST OF YOUR IRON MAN ARMOR?
LONG STORY. YOU WERE GONE A WHILE.
T'CHALLA, YOU NEED TO GET OUT OF THERE!
IT'S HIM! HE'S ON HIS WAY!
COPY, BLACK WIDOW.
QUESTION FOR YOU, CAPTAIN...

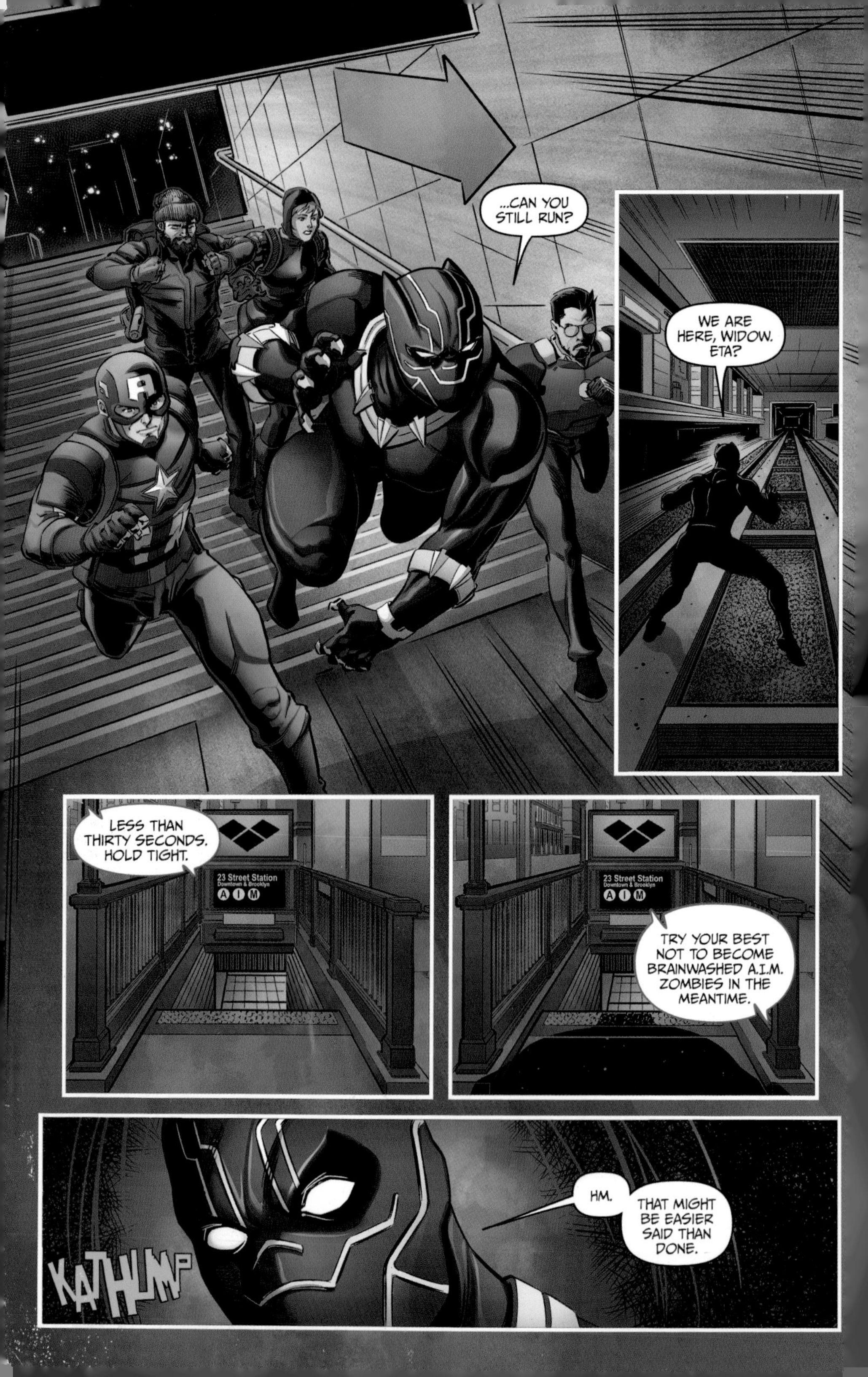
...CAN YOU STILL RUN?
WE ARE HERE, WIDOW. ETA?
LESS THAN THIRTY SECONDS. HOLD TIGHT.
23 Street Station
Downtown & Brooklyn
A I M
23 Street Station
Downtown & Brooklyn
A I M
TRY YOUR BEST NOT TO BECOME BRAINWASHED A.I.M. ZOMBIES IN THE MEANTIME.
HM.
THAT MIGHT BE EASIER SAID THAN DONE.
KATHUMP

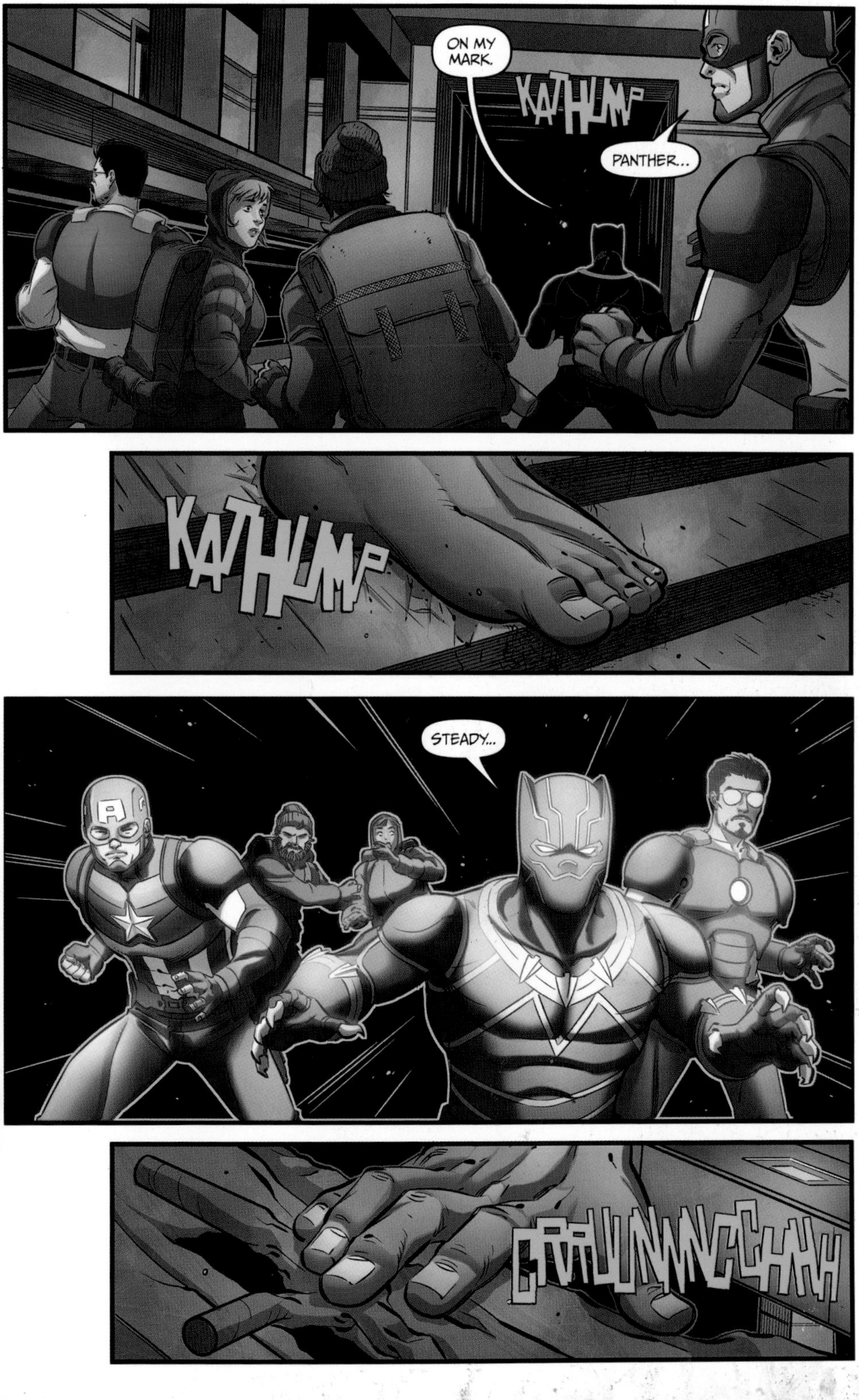
ON MY MARK.
KATHUMP
PANTHER...
KATHUMP
STEADY...
CRRUNNNCCHHH

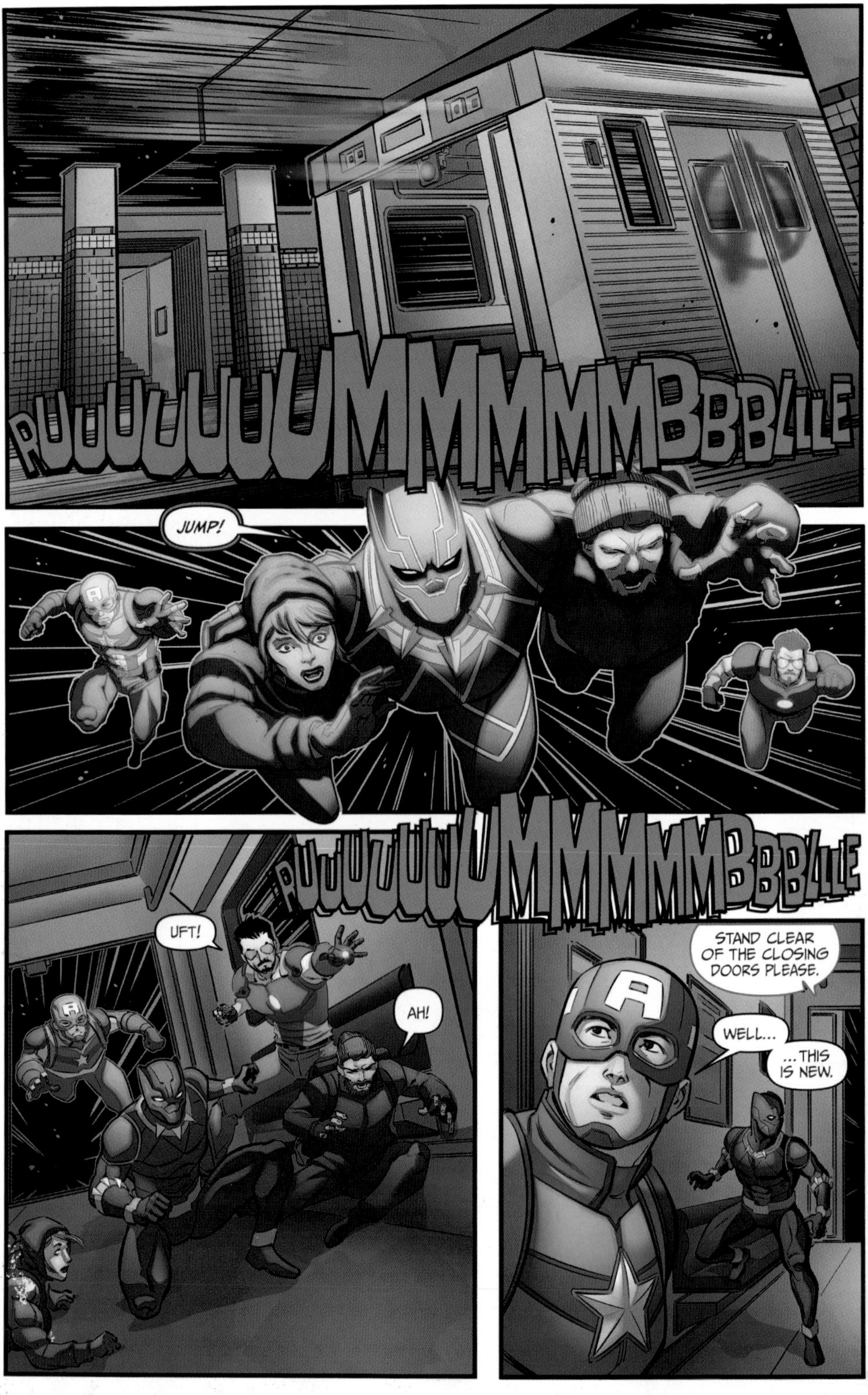
RUUUUUUUMMMMMMBBBLLLE
JUMP!
RUUUUUUUMMMMMMBBBLLLE
UFT!
AH!
STAND CLEAR OF THE CLOSING DOORS PLEASE.
WELL...
...THIS IS NEW.

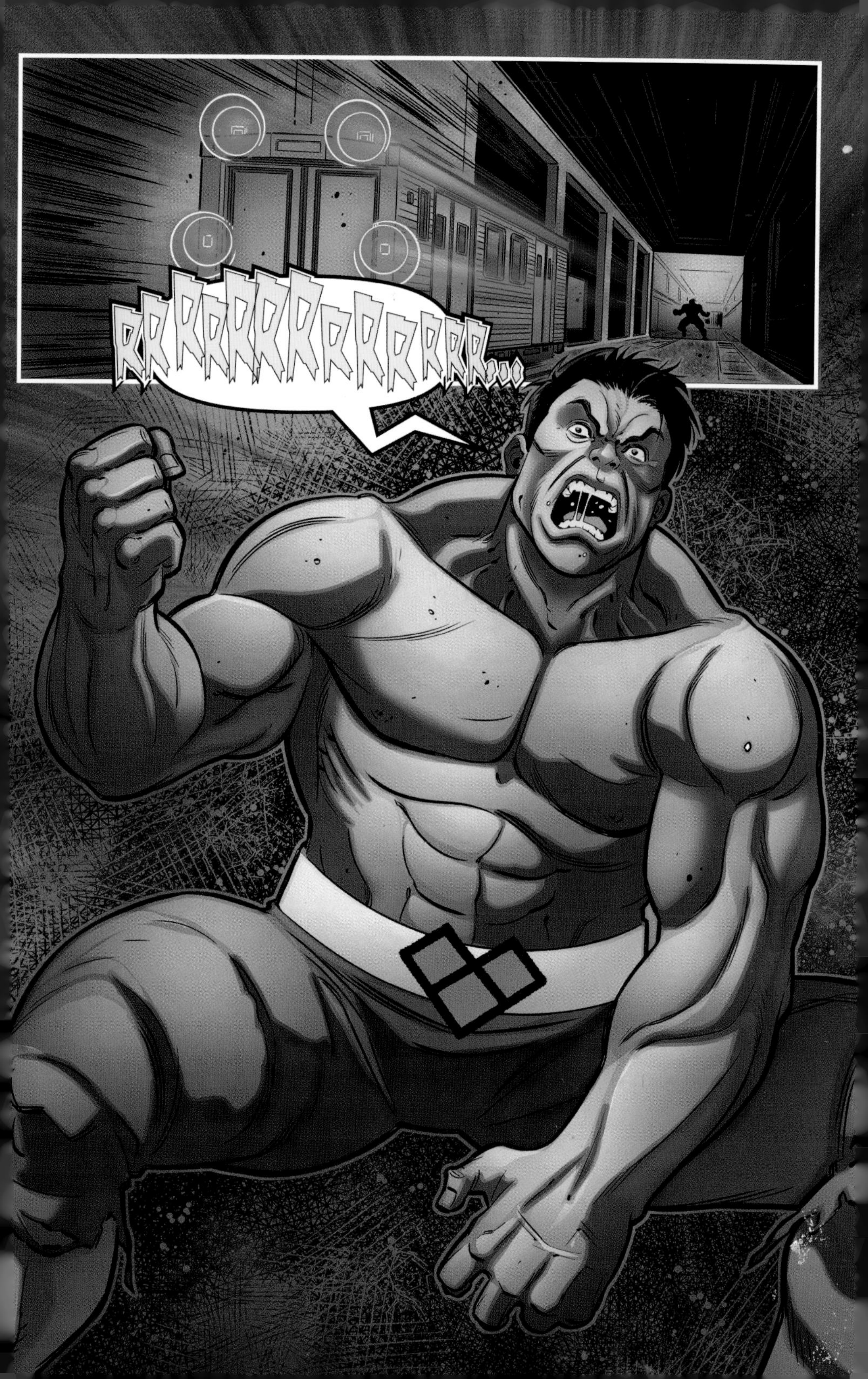
RRRRRRRRRRRRR...

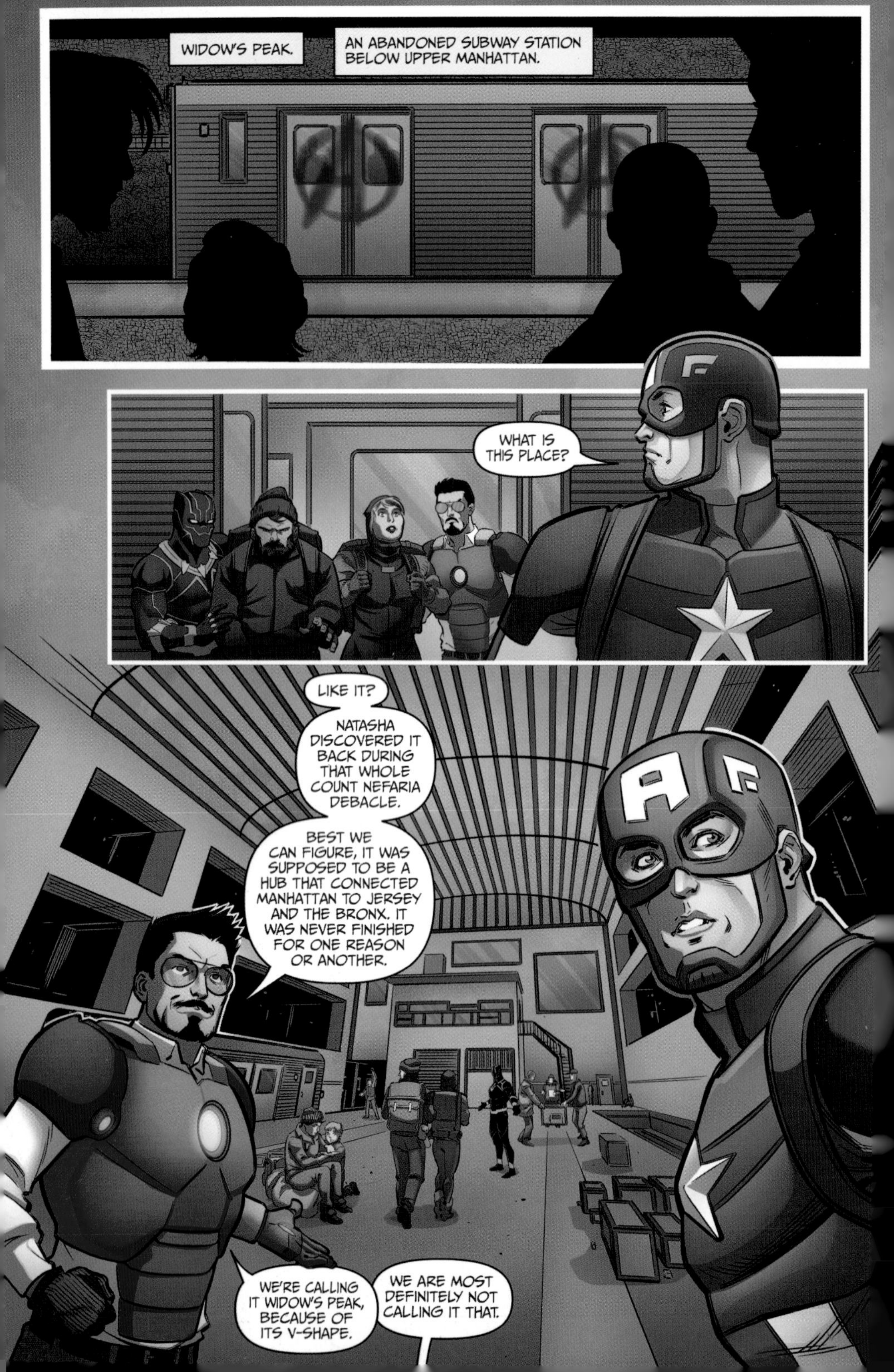
WIDOW'S PEAK.
AN ABANDONED SUBWAY STATION BELOW UPPER MANHATTAN.
WHAT IS THIS PLACE?
LIKE IT?
NATASHA DISCOVERED IT BACK DURING THAT WHOLE COUNT NEFARIA DEBACLE.
BEST WE CAN FIGURE, IT WAS SUPPOSED TO BE A HUB THAT CONNECTED MANHATTAN TO JERSEY AND THE BRONX. IT WAS NEVER FINISHED FOR ONE REASON OR ANOTHER.
WE'RE CALLING IT WIDOW'S PEAK, BECAUSE OF ITS V-SHAPE.
WE ARE MOST DEFINITELY NOT CALLING IT THAT.

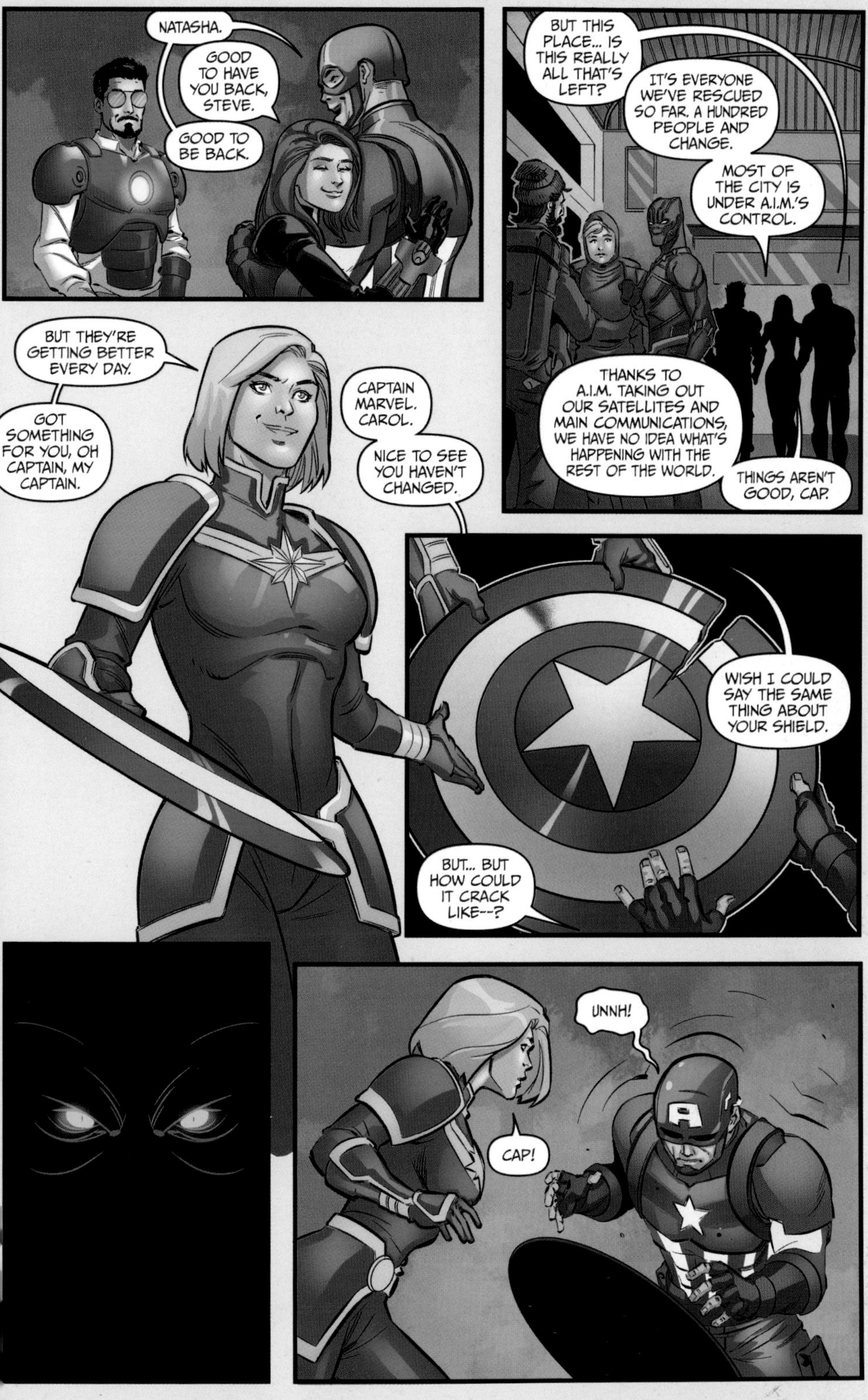
NATASHA.
GOOD TO HAVE YOU BACK, STEVE.
GOOD TO BE BACK.
BUT THIS PLACE... IS THIS REALLY ALL THAT'S LEFT?
IT'S EVERYONE WE'VE RESCUED SO FAR. A HUNDRED PEOPLE AND CHANGE.
MOST OF THE CITY IS UNDER A.I.M.'S CONTROL.
THANKS TO A.I.M. TAKING OUT OUR SATELLITES AND MAIN COMMUNICATIONS, WE HAVE NO IDEA WHAT'S HAPPENING WITH THE REST OF THE WORLD.
THINGS AREN'T GOOD, CAP.
BUT THEY'RE GETTING BETTER EVERY DAY.
GOT SOMETHING FOR YOU, OH CAPTAIN, MY CAPTAIN.
CAPTAIN MARVEL. CAROL.
NICE TO SEE YOU HAVEN'T CHANGED.
WISH I COULD SAY THE SAME THING ABOUT YOUR SHIELD.
BUT... BUT HOW COULD IT CRACK LIKE--?
UNNH!
CAP!

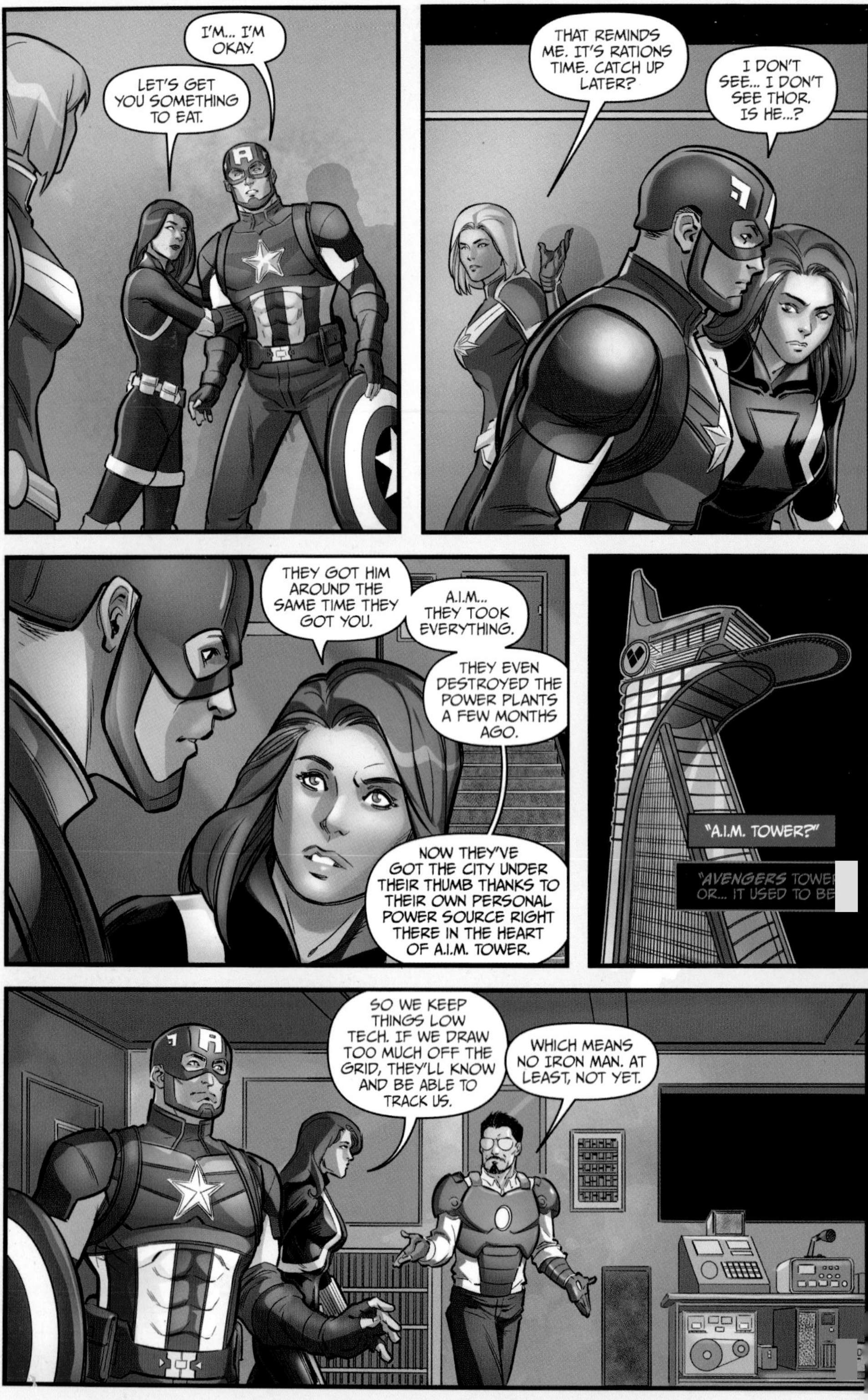
LET'S GET YOU SOMETHING TO EAT.
I'M... I'M OKAY.
THAT REMINDS ME. IT'S RATIONS TIME. CATCH UP LATER?
I DON'T SEE... I DON'T SEE THOR. IS HE...?
THEY GOT HIM AROUND THE SAME TIME THEY GOT YOU.
A.I.M... THEY TOOK EVERYTHING.
THEY EVEN DESTROYED THE POWER PLANTS A FEW MONTHS AGO.
NOW THEY'VE GOT THE CITY UNDER THEIR THUMB THANKS TO THEIR OWN PERSONAL POWER SOURCE RIGHT THERE IN THE HEART OF A.I.M. TOWER.
"A.I.M. TOWER?"
"AVENGERS TOWE
OR... IT USED TO BE
SO WE KEEP THINGS LOW TECH. IF WE DRAW TOO MUCH OFF THE GRID, THEY'LL KNOW AND BE ABLE TO TRACK US.
WHICH MEANS NO IRON MAN. AT LEAST, NOT YET.

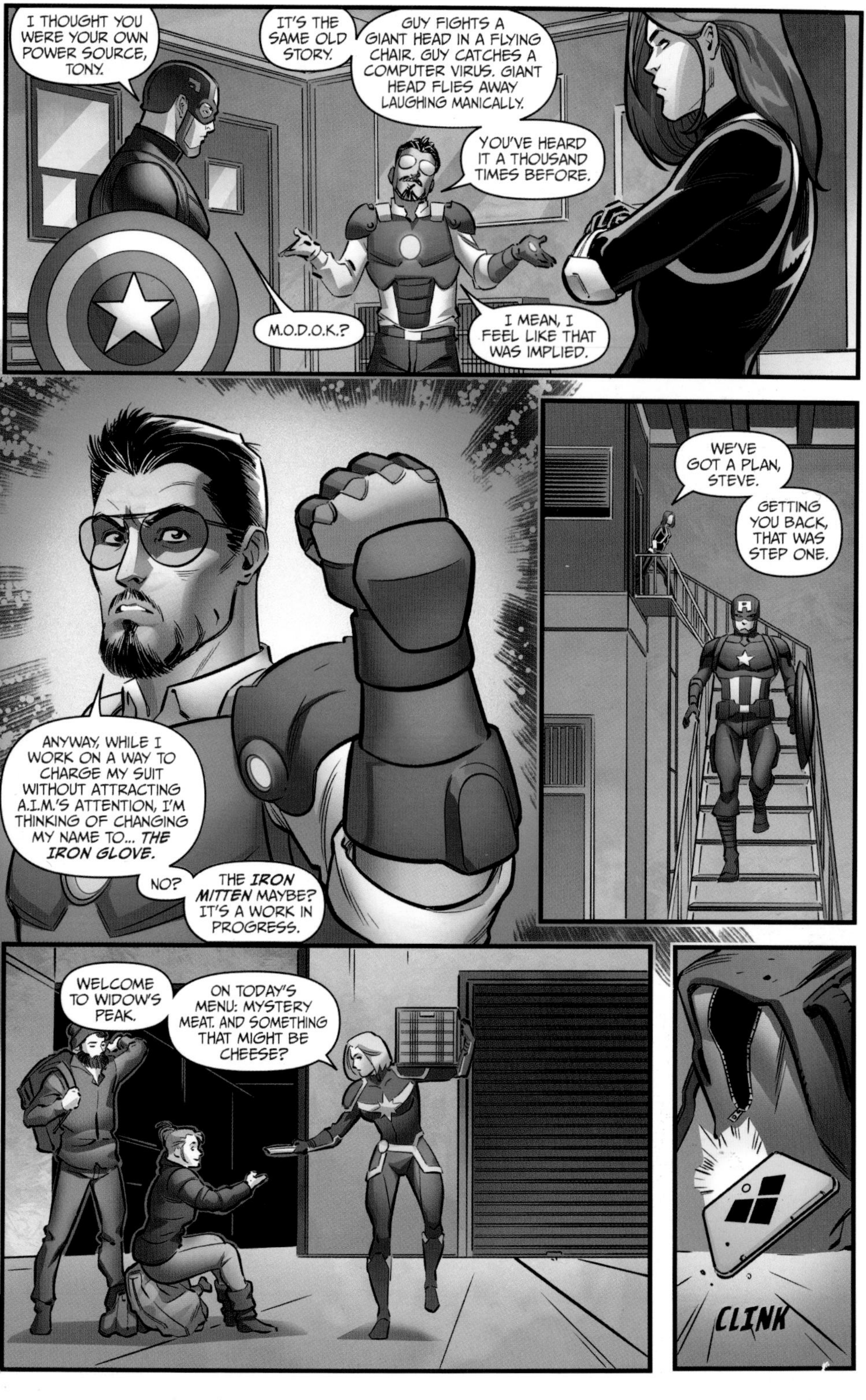

I THOUGHT YOU WERE YOUR OWN POWER SOURCE, TONY.
IT'S THE SAME OLD STORY.
GUY FIGHTS A GIANT HEAD IN A FLYING CHAIR. GUY CATCHES A COMPUTER VIRUS. GIANT HEAD FLIES AWAY LAUGHING MANICALLY.
YOU'VE HEARD IT A THOUSAND TIMES BEFORE.
M.O.D.O.K.?
I MEAN, I FEEL LIKE THAT WAS IMPLIED.
ANYWAY, WHILE I WORK ON A WAY TO CHARGE MY SUIT WITHOUT ATTRACTING A.I.M.'S ATTENTION, I'M THINKING OF CHANGING MY NAME TO... THE IRON GLOVE.
NO?
THE IRON MITTEN MAYBE? IT'S A WORK IN PROGRESS.
WE'VE GOT A PLAN, STEVE.
GETTING YOU BACK, THAT WAS STEP ONE.
WELCOME TO WIDOW'S PEAK.
ON TODAY'S MENU: MYSTERY MEAT. AND SOMETHING THAT MIGHT BE CHEESE?
CLINK

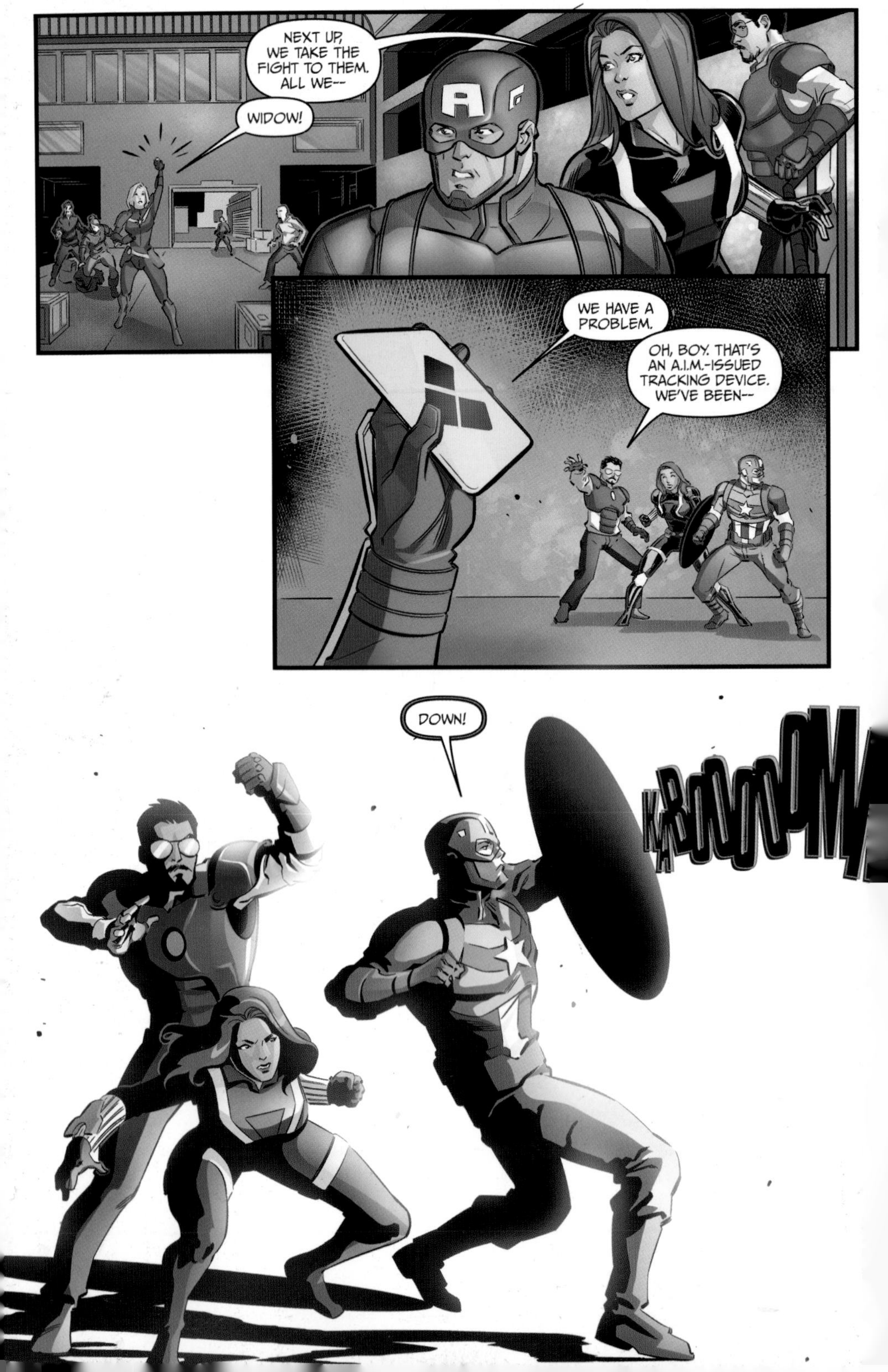
NEXT UP, WE TAKE THE FIGHT TO THEM. ALL WE--
WIDOW!
WE HAVE A PROBLEM.
OH, BOY. THAT'S AN A.I.M.-ISSUED TRACKING DEVICE. WE'VE BEEN--
DOWN!
KABOOOOOOM

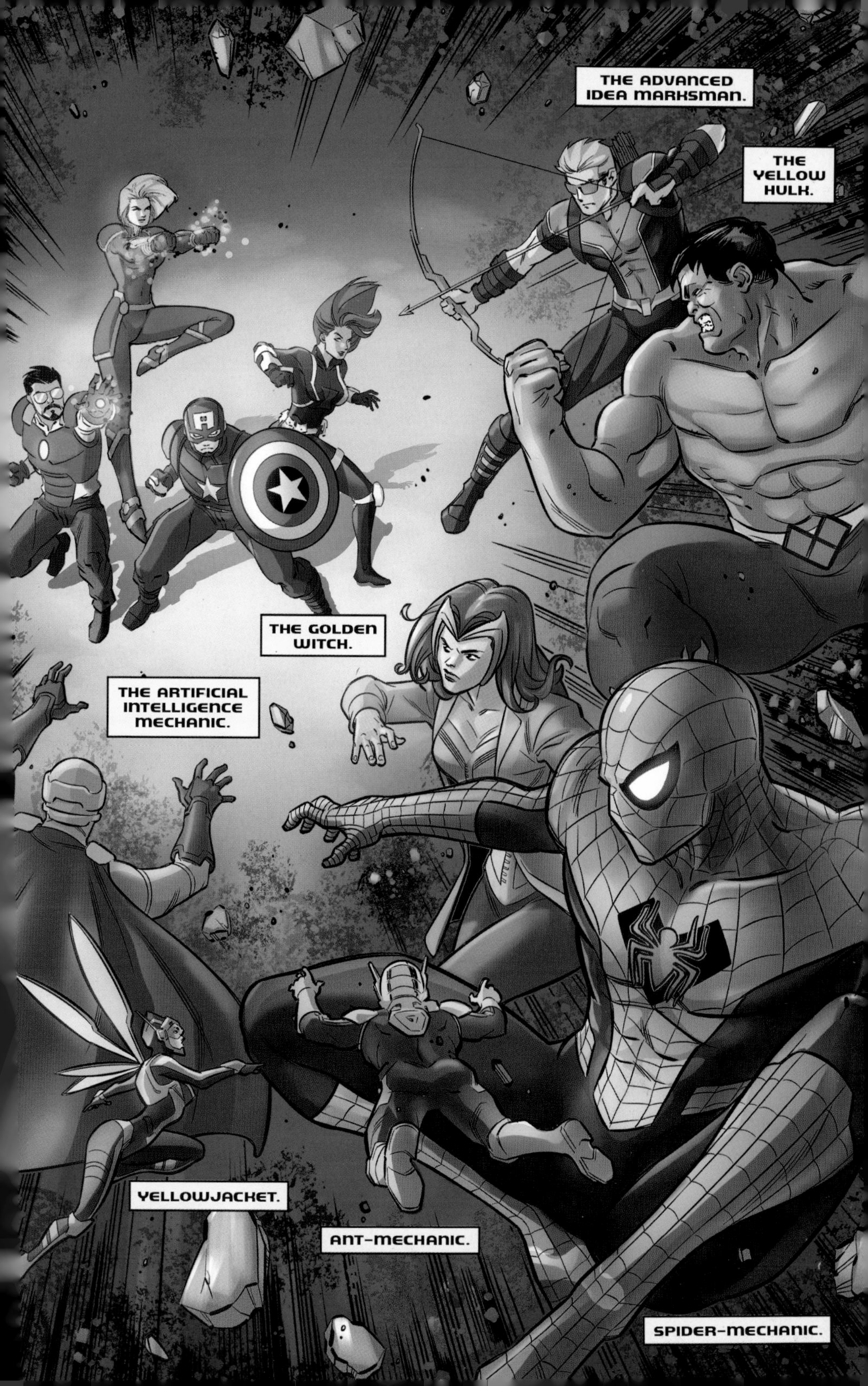
THE ADVANCED IDEA MARKSMAN.
THE YELLOW HULK.
THE GOLDEN WITCH.
THE ARTIFICIAL INTELLIGENCE MECHANIC.
YELLOWJACKET.
ANT-MECHANIC.
SPIDER-MECHANIC.

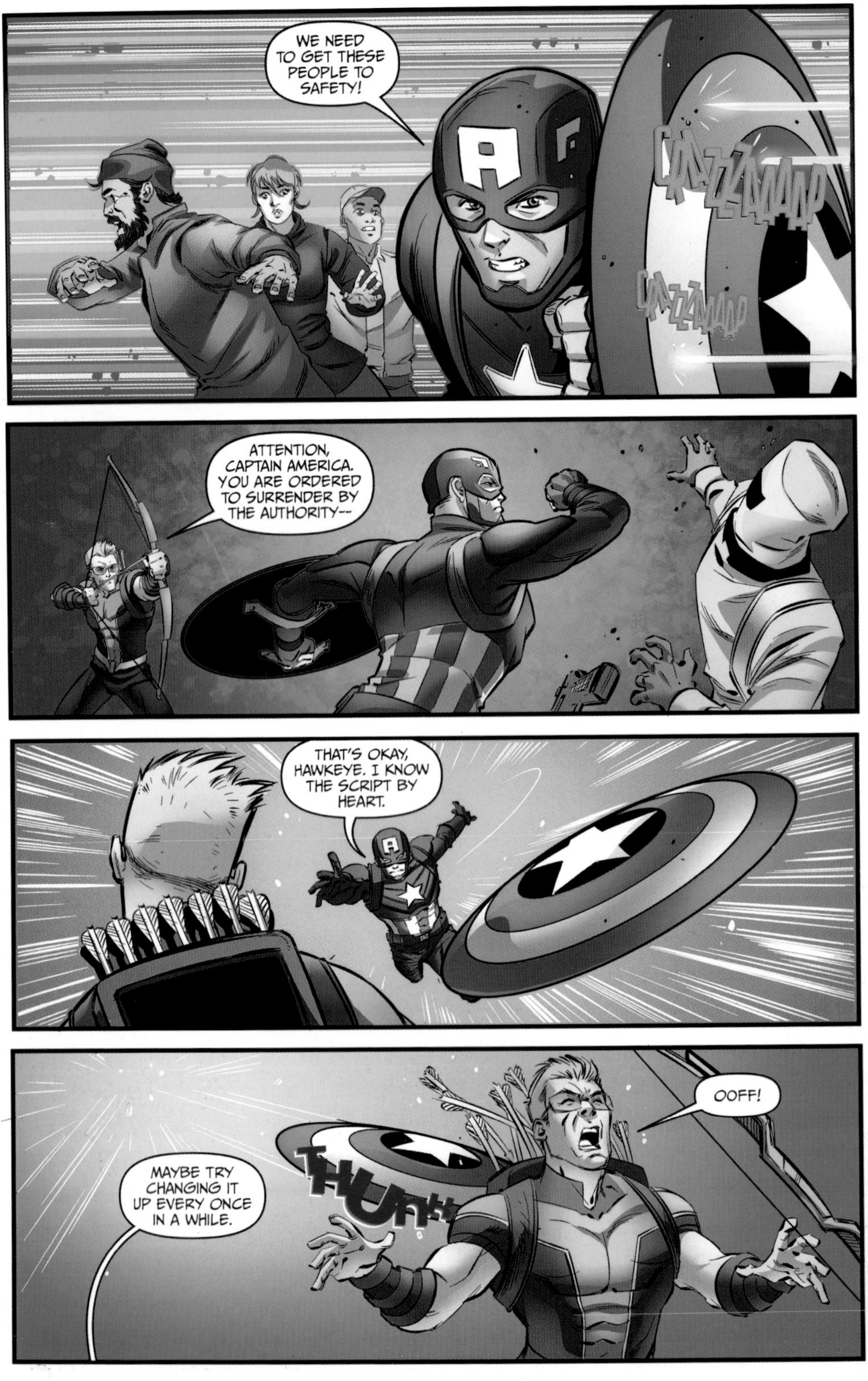

WE NEED TO GET THESE PEOPLE TO SAFETY!
ATTENTION, CAPTAIN AMERICA. YOU ARE ORDERED TO SURRENDER BY THE AUTHORITY--
THAT'S OKAY, HAWKEYE. I KNOW THE SCRIPT BY HEART.
THUNK
OOFF!
MAYBE TRY CHANGING IT UP EVERY ONCE IN A WHILE.

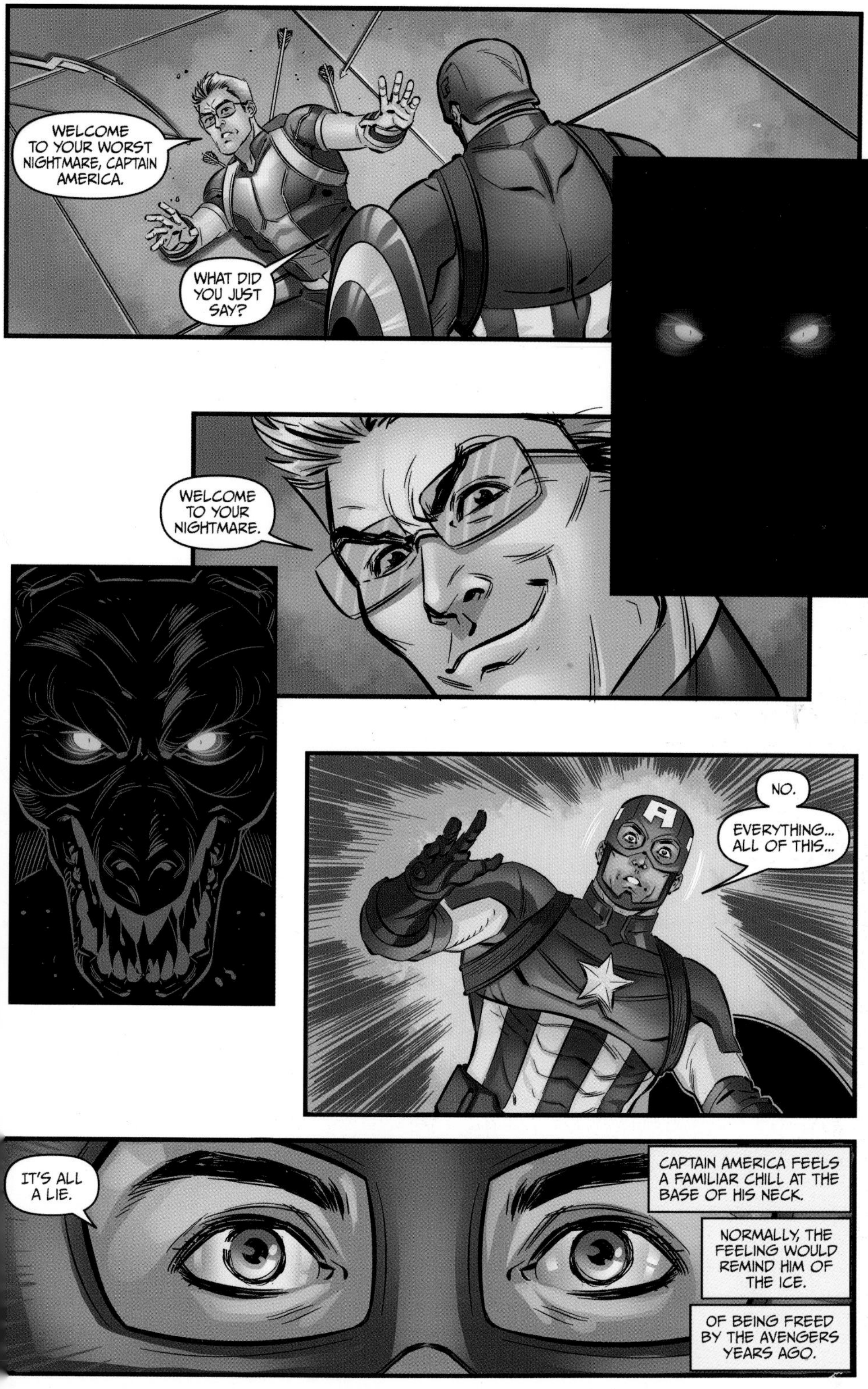
WELCOME TO YOUR WORST NIGHTMARE, CAPTAIN AMERICA.
WHAT DID YOU JUST SAY?
WELCOME TO YOUR NIGHTMARE.
NO.
EVERYTHING... ALL OF THIS...
IT'S ALL A LIE.
CAPTAIN AMERICA FEELS A FAMILIAR CHILL AT THE BASE OF HIS NECK.
NORMALLY, THE FEELING WOULD REMIND HIM OF THE ICE.
OF BEING FREED BY THE AVENGERS YEARS AGO.

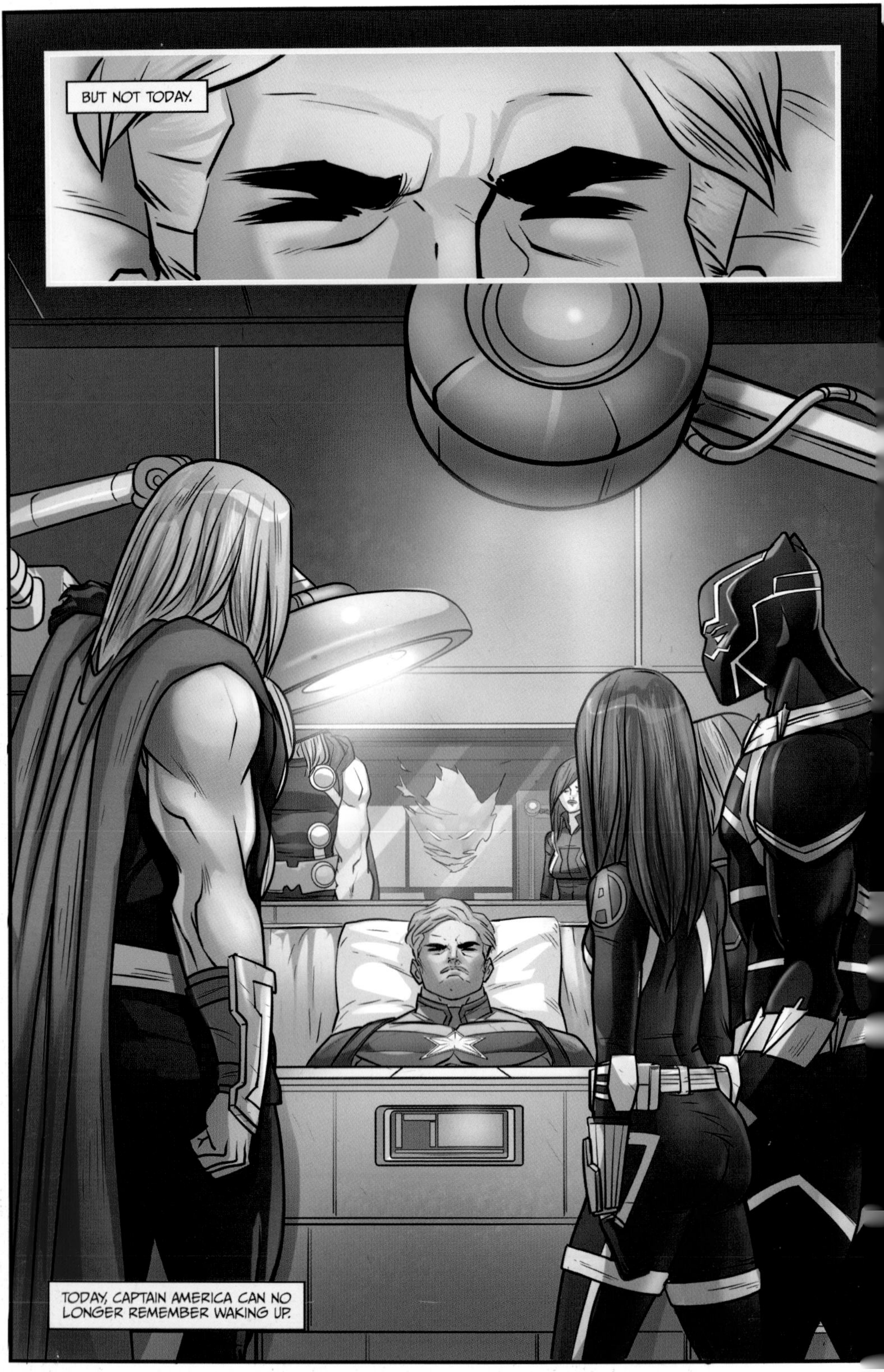
BUT NOT TODAY.
TODAY, CAPTAIN AMERICA CAN NO LONGER REMEMBER WAKING UP.

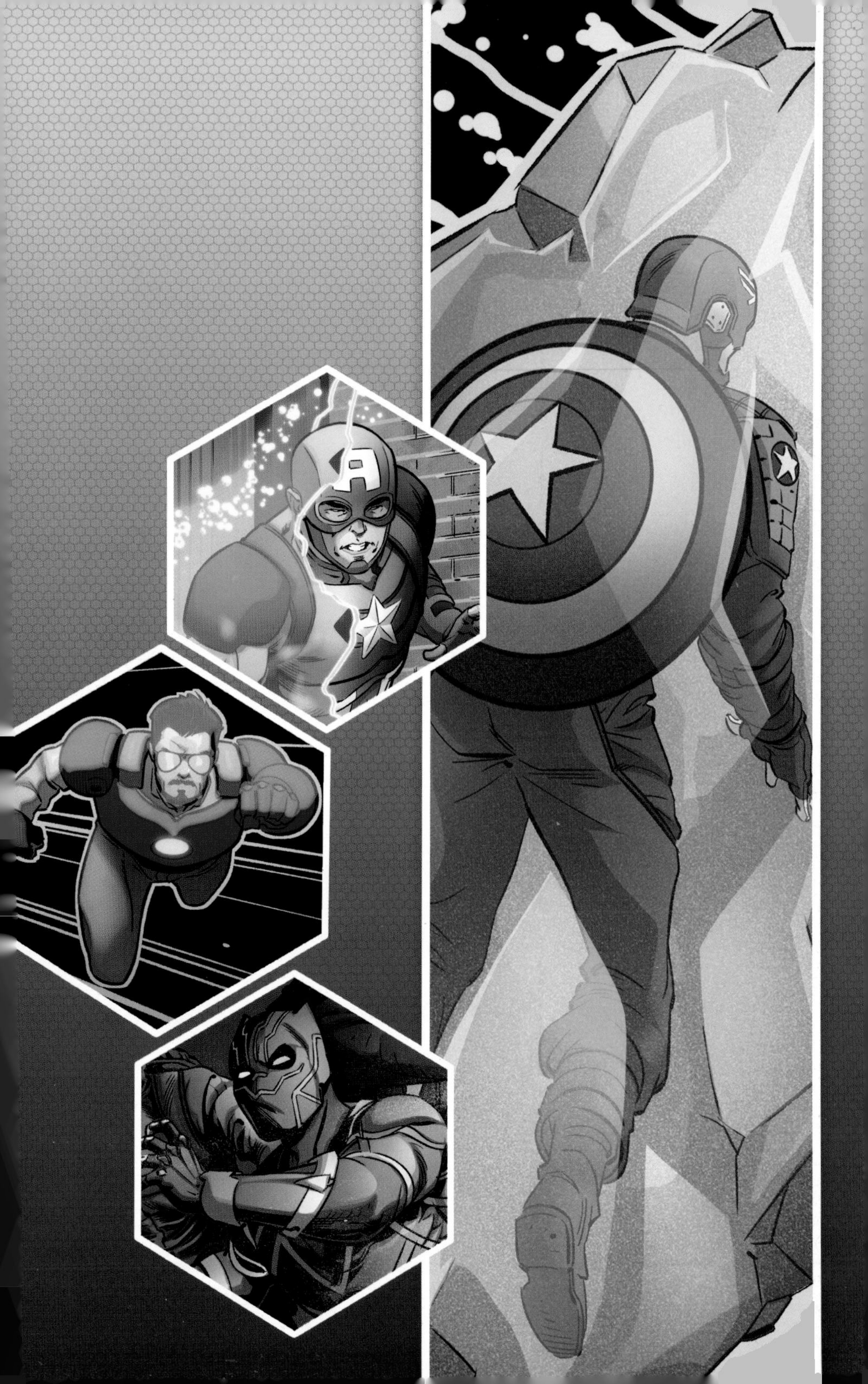

ART BY: JON SOMMARIVA
COLORS BY: PAC23

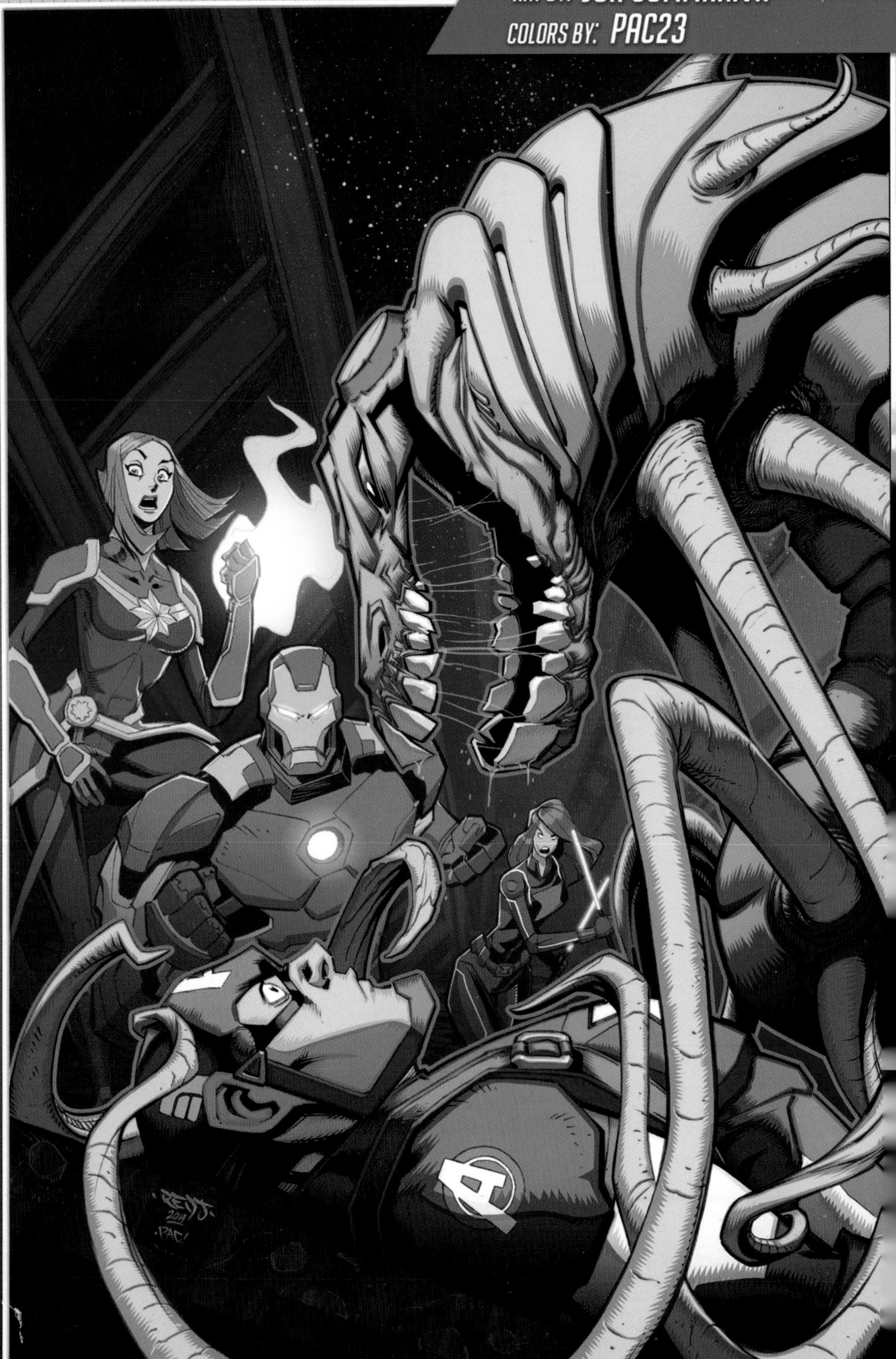

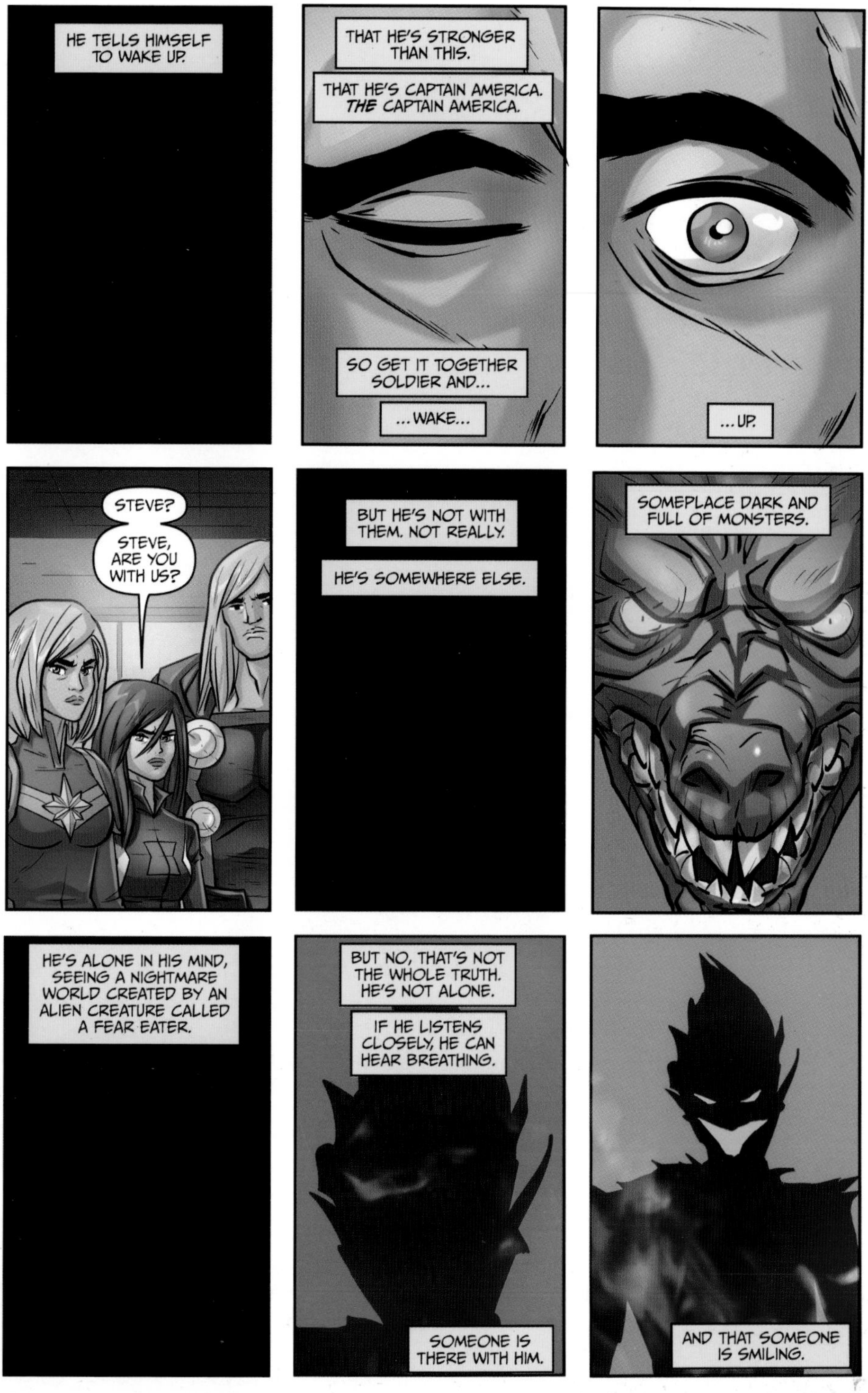
HE TELLS HIMSELF TO WAKE UP.
THAT HE'S STRONGER THAN THIS.
THAT HE'S CAPTAIN AMERICA. *THE* CAPTAIN AMERICA.
SO GET IT TOGETHER SOLDIER AND...
...WAKE...
...UP.
STEVE?
STEVE, ARE YOU WITH US?
BUT HE'S NOT WITH THEM. NOT REALLY.
HE'S SOMEWHERE ELSE.
SOMEPLACE DARK AND FULL OF MONSTERS.
HE'S ALONE IN HIS MIND, SEEING A NIGHTMARE WORLD CREATED BY AN ALIEN CREATURE CALLED A FEAR EATER.
BUT NO, THAT'S NOT THE WHOLE TRUTH. HE'S NOT ALONE.
IF HE LISTENS CLOSELY, HE CAN HEAR BREATHING.
SOMEONE IS THERE WITH HIM.
AND THAT SOMEONE IS SMILING.

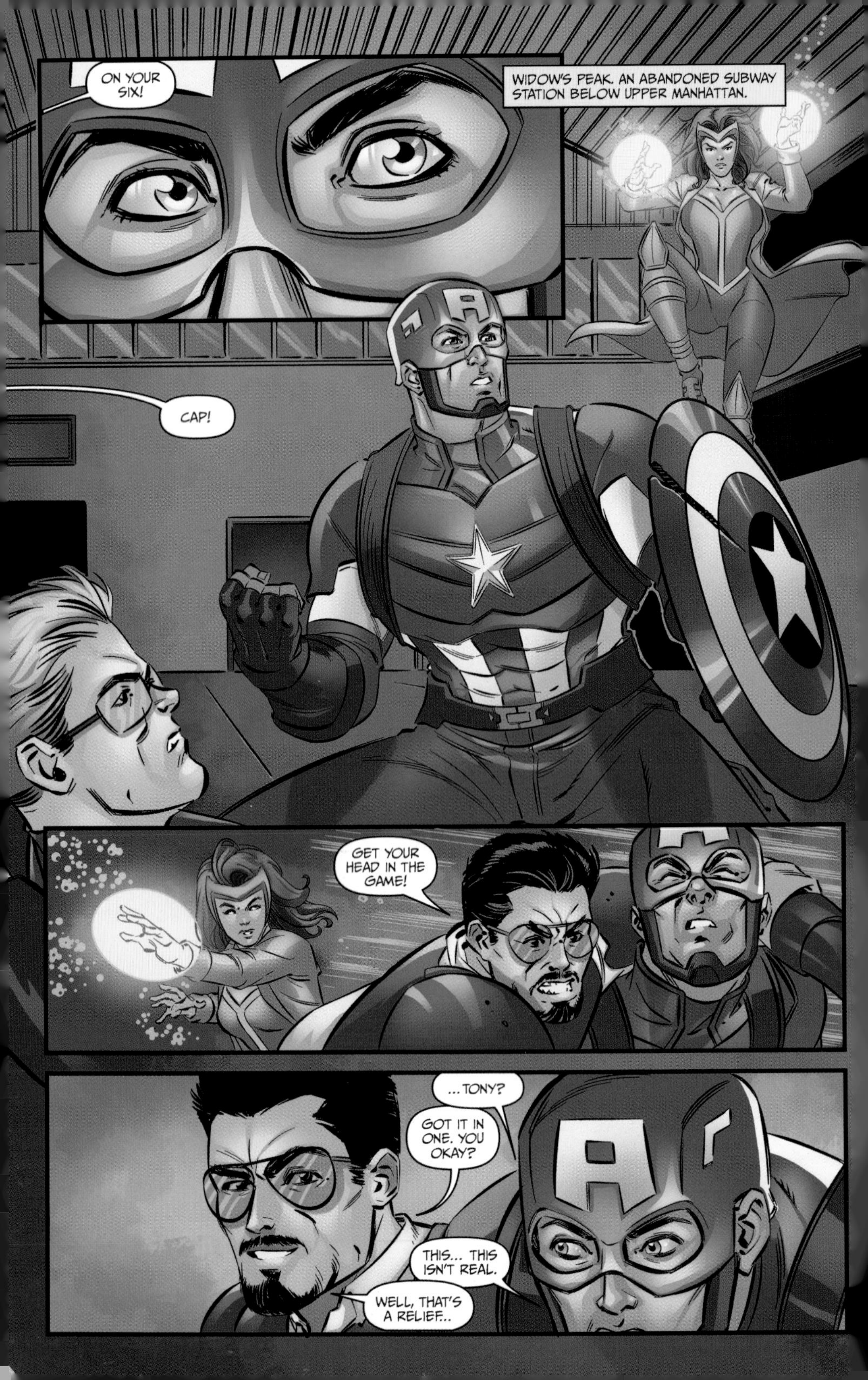
ON YOUR SIX!
WIDOW'S PEAK. AN ABANDONED SUBWAY STATION BELOW UPPER MANHATTAN.
CAP!
GET YOUR HEAD IN THE GAME!
...TONY?
GOT IT IN ONE. YOU OKAY?
THIS... THIS ISN'T REAL.
WELL, THAT'S A RELIEF...

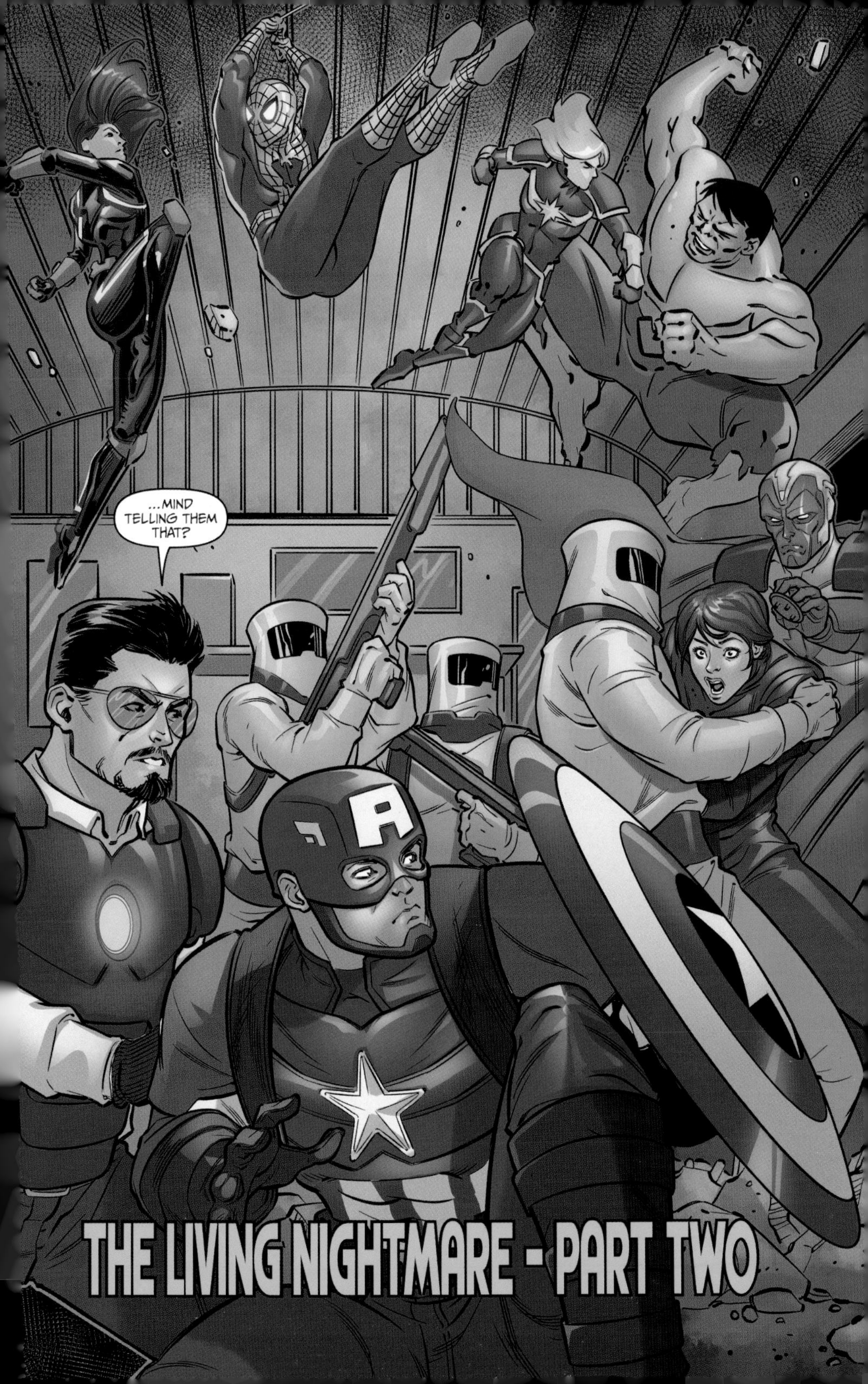
...MIND TELLING THEM THAT?
THE LIVING NIGHTMARE - PART TWO

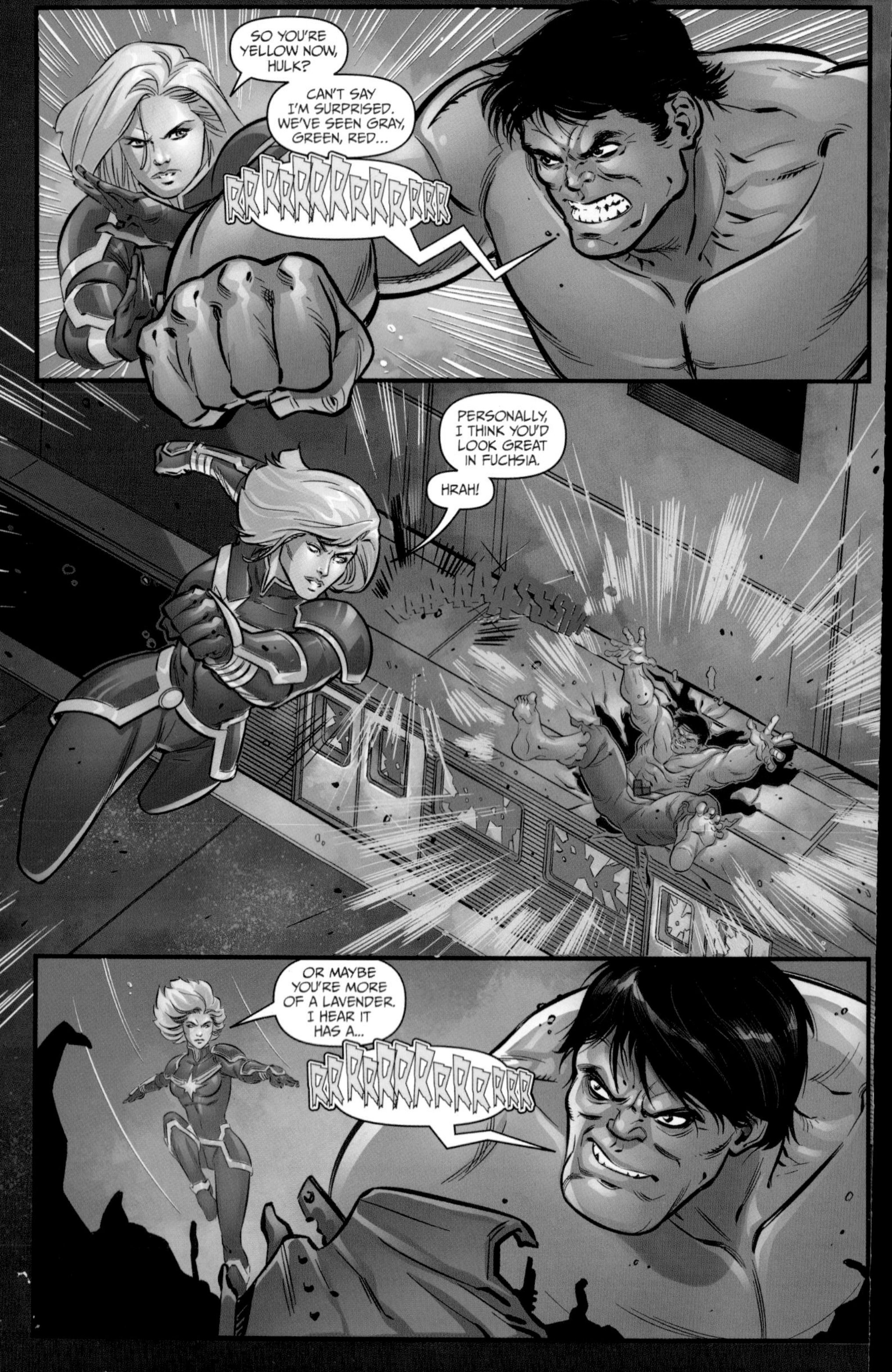
SO YOU'RE YELLOW NOW, HULK?
CAN'T SAY I'M SURPRISED. WE'VE SEEN GRAY, GREEN, RED...
PERSONALLY, I THINK YOU'D LOOK GREAT IN FUCHSIA.
HRAH!
OR MAYBE YOU'RE MORE OF A LAVENDER. I HEAR IT HAS A...

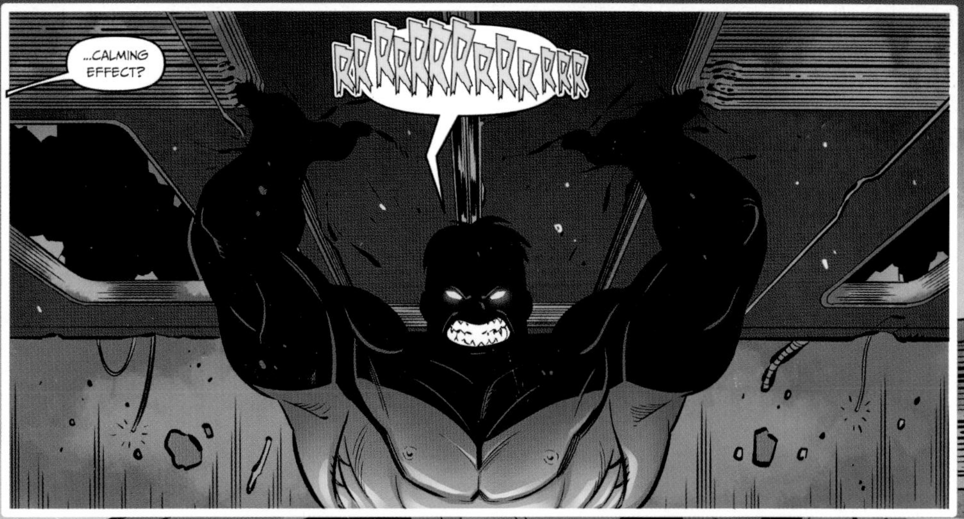
...CALMING EFFECT?
RRRRRRRRRRRRRR

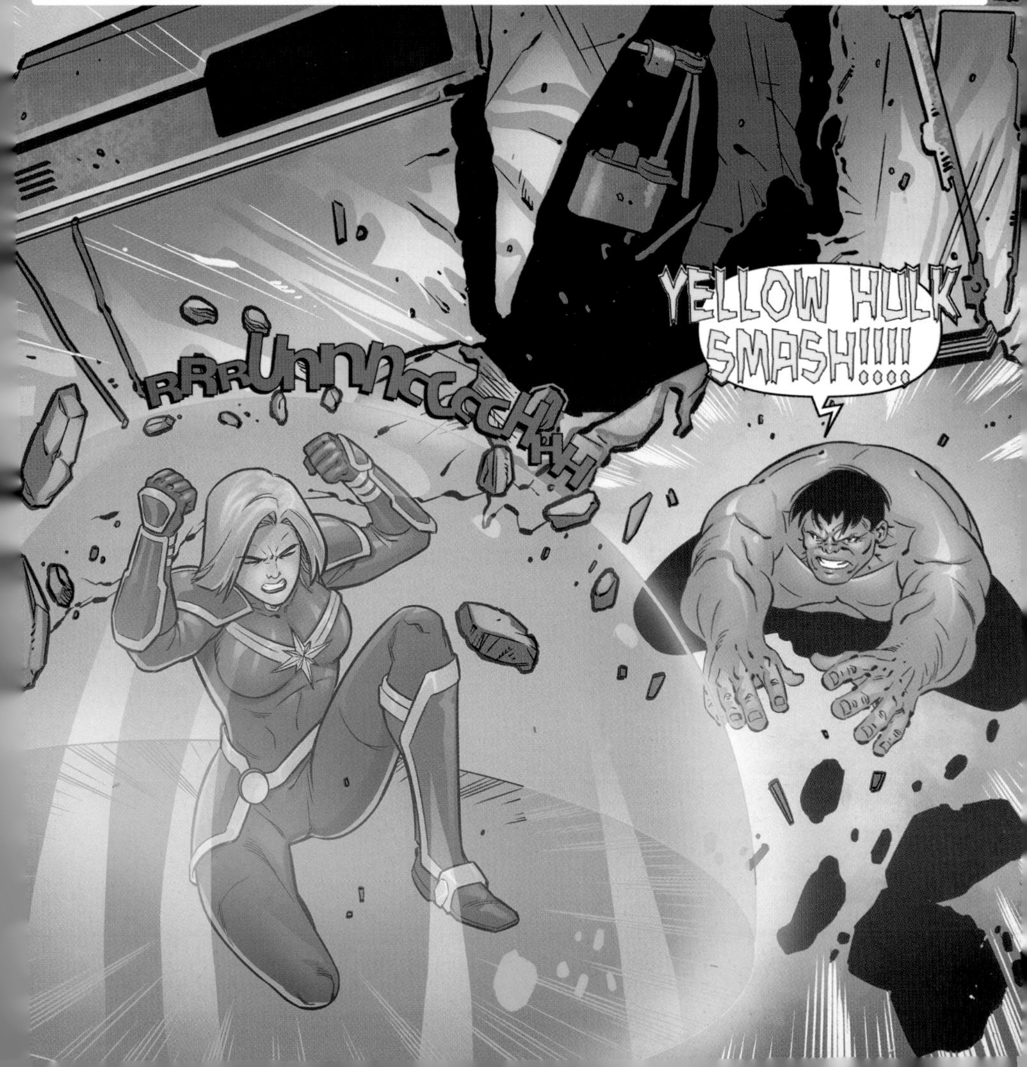
RRRUNNNCCCCHHHH
YELLOW HULK SMASH!!!!

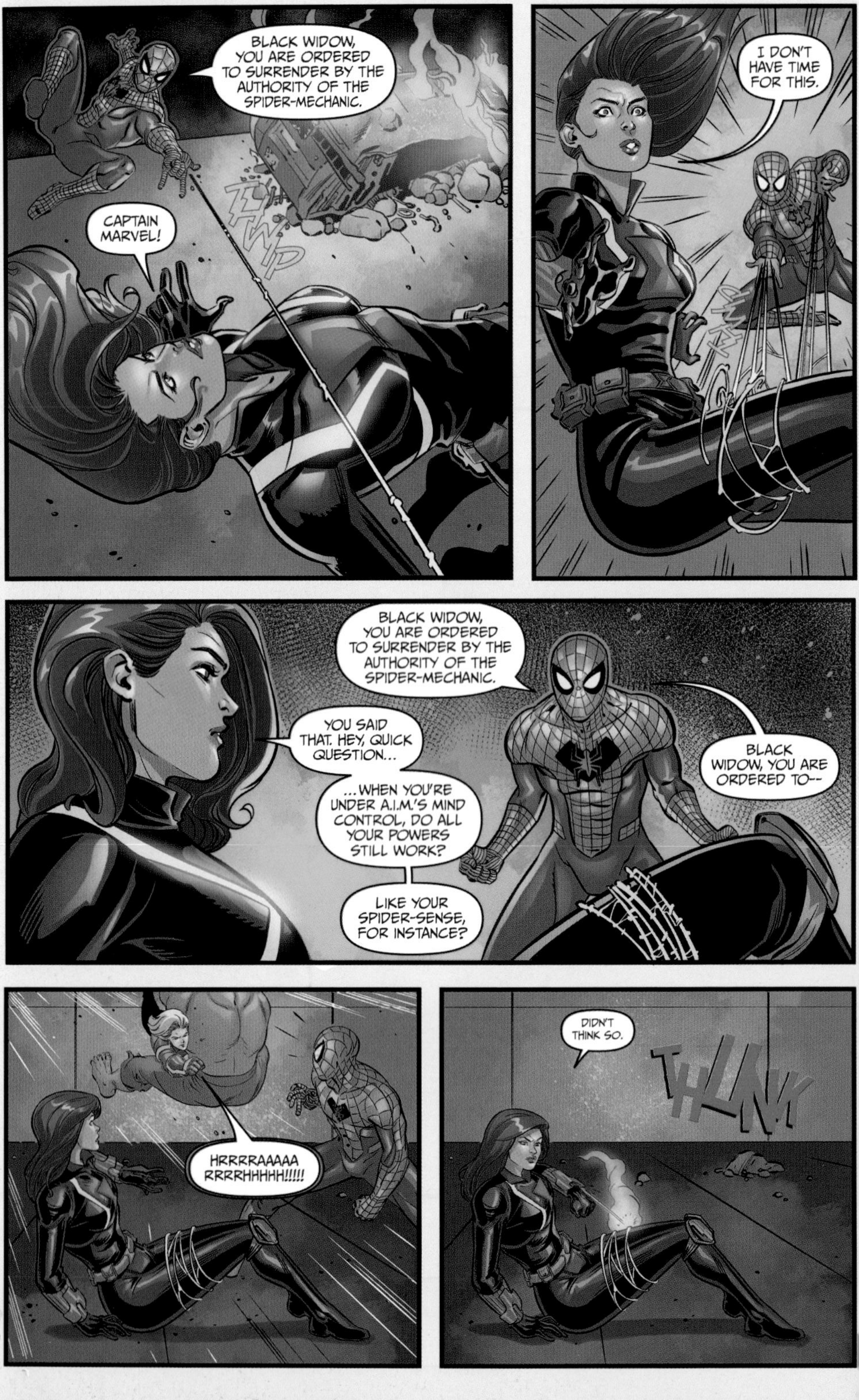
BLACK WIDOW, YOU ARE ORDERED TO SURRENDER BY THE AUTHORITY OF THE SPIDER-MECHANIC.
CAPTAIN MARVEL!
I DON'T HAVE TIME FOR THIS.
BLACK WIDOW, YOU ARE ORDERED TO SURRENDER BY THE AUTHORITY OF THE SPIDER-MECHANIC.
YOU SAID THAT. HEY, QUICK QUESTION...
...WHEN YOU'RE UNDER A.I.M.'S MIND CONTROL, DO ALL YOUR POWERS STILL WORK?
LIKE YOUR SPIDER-SENSE, FOR INSTANCE?
BLACK WIDOW, YOU ARE ORDERED TO--
HRRRRAAAAA RRRRHHHHH!!!!!
DIDN'T THINK SO.
THUNK

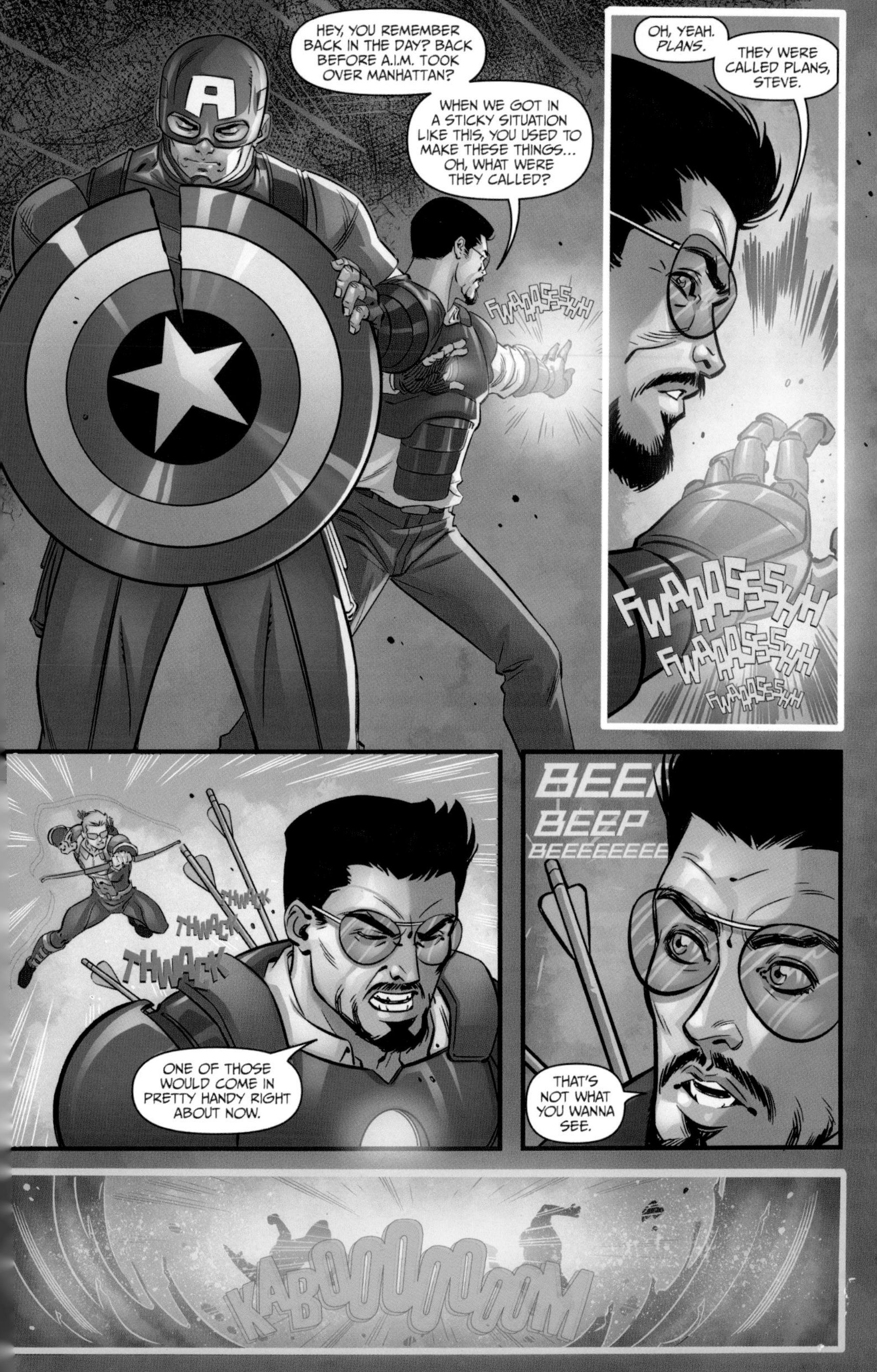
HEY, YOU REMEMBER BACK IN THE DAY? BACK BEFORE A.I.M. TOOK OVER MANHATTAN?
WHEN WE GOT IN A STICKY SITUATION LIKE THIS, YOU USED TO MAKE THESE THINGS... OH, WHAT WERE THEY CALLED?
FWAAASSSHH
OH, YEAH. *PLANS.*
THEY WERE CALLED PLANS, STEVE.
FWAAASSSHH
FWAAASSSHH
FWAAASSSHH
THWACK
THWACK
THWACK
ONE OF THOSE WOULD COME IN PRETTY HANDY RIGHT ABOUT NOW.
BEEP
BEEEEEEEE
THAT'S NOT WHAT YOU WANNA SEE.
KABOOOOOOOOM

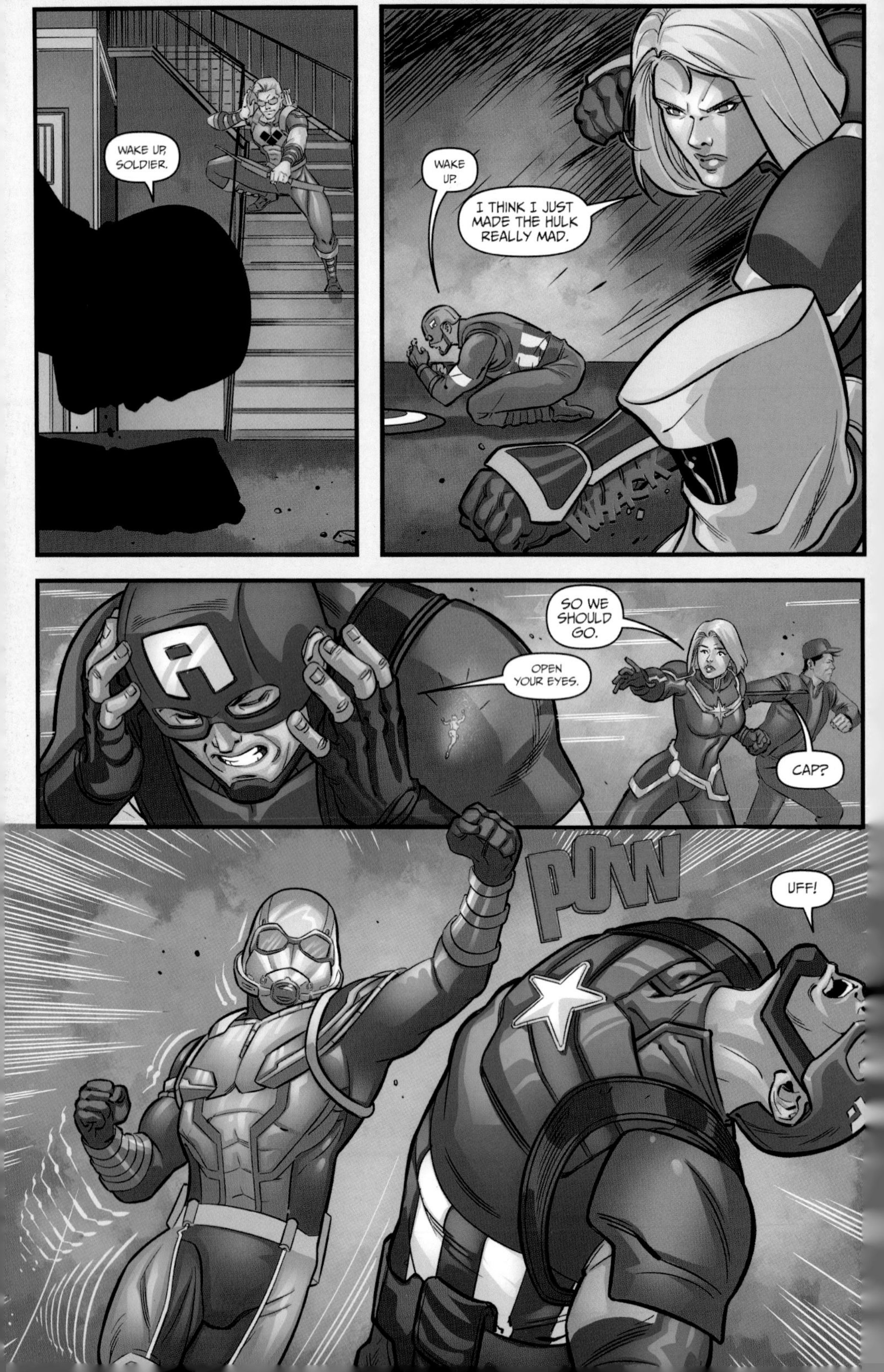

WAKE UP, SOLDIER.
WAKE UP.
I THINK I JUST MADE THE HULK REALLY MAD.
WHACK
SO WE SHOULD GO.
OPEN YOUR EYES.
CAP?
POW
UFF!

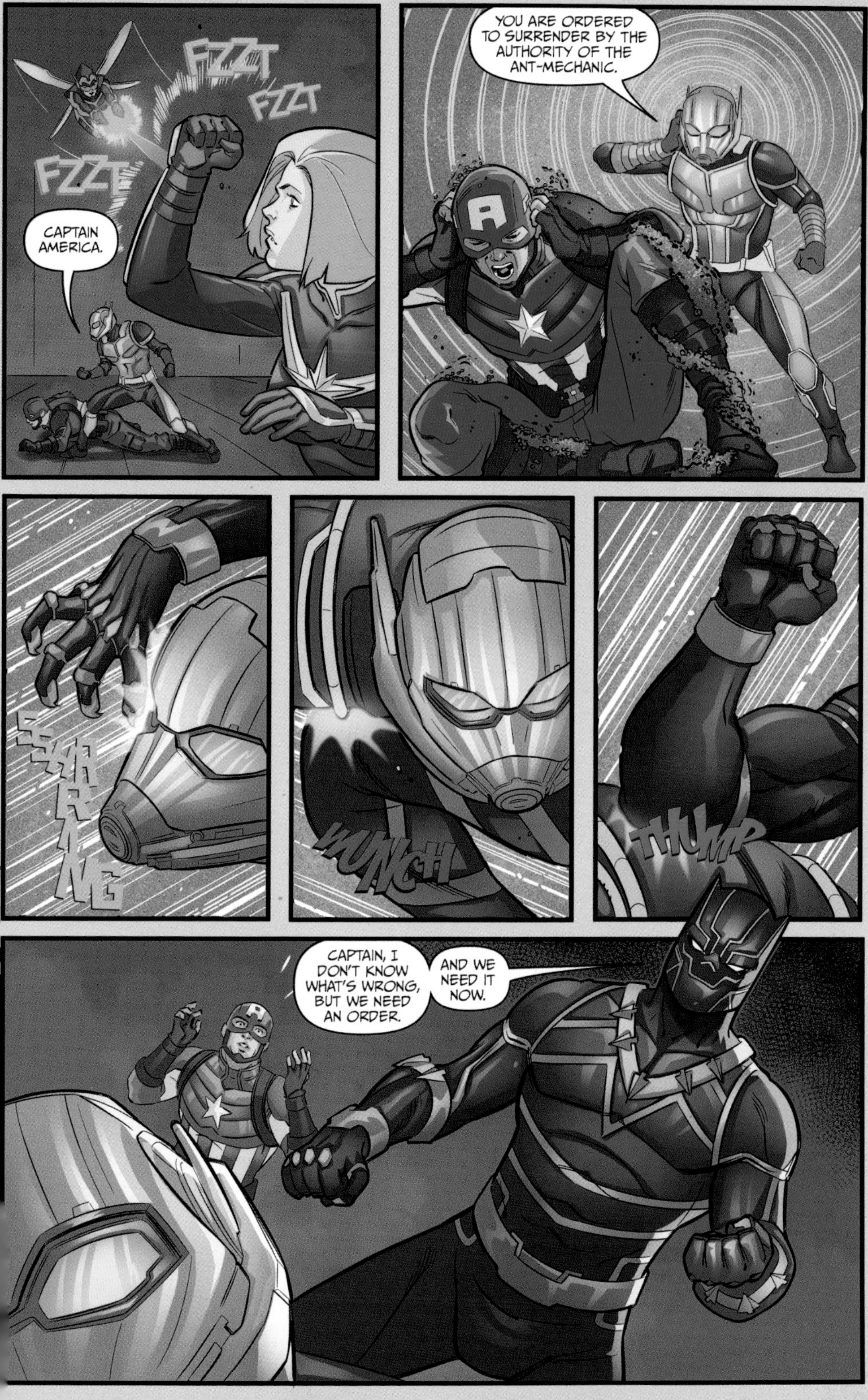
FZZT
FZZT
FZZT
CAPTAIN AMERICA.
YOU ARE ORDERED TO SURRENDER BY THE AUTHORITY OF THE ANT-MECHANIC.
SSHRRANG
WUNCH
THUMP
CAPTAIN, I DON'T KNOW WHAT'S WRONG, BUT WE NEED AN ORDER.
AND WE NEED IT NOW.

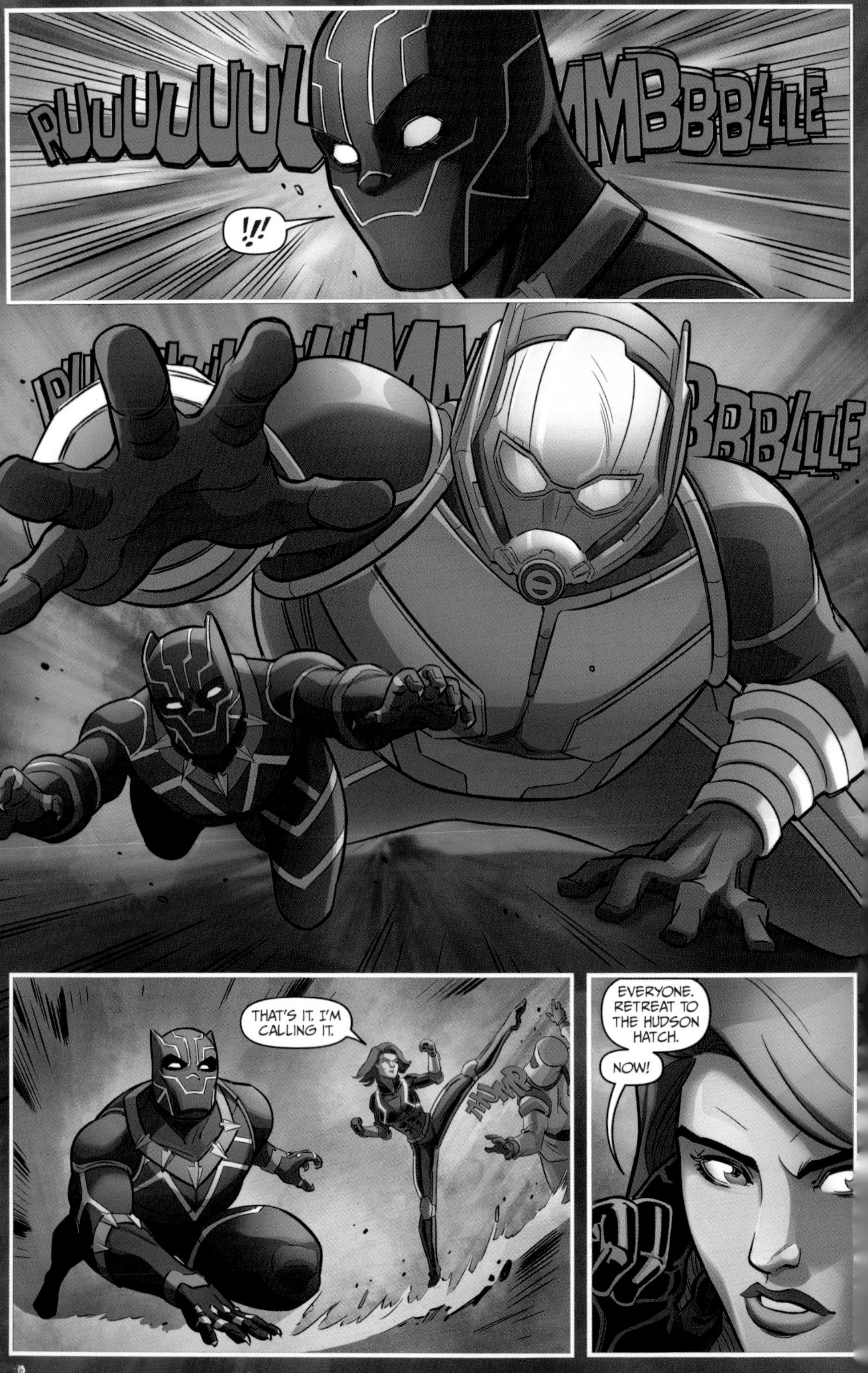
RUUUUUUMMBBBLLLE
!!!
RUUUUUUMMMBBBLLLE
THAT'S IT. I'M CALLING IT.
THUMP
EVERYONE. RETREAT TO THE HUDSON HATCH.
NOW!

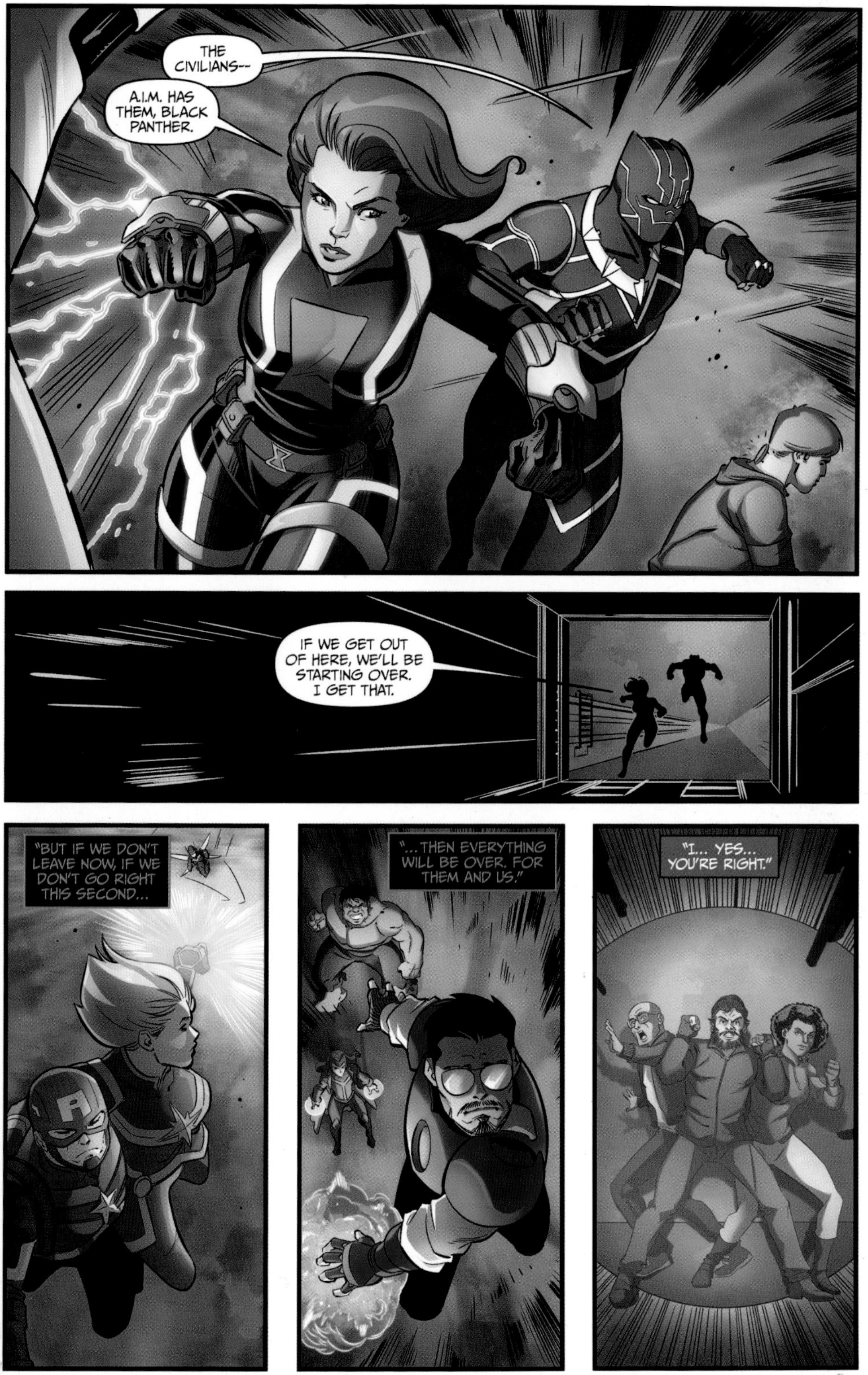
THE CIVILIANS--
A.I.M. HAS THEM, BLACK PANTHER.
IF WE GET OUT OF HERE, WE'LL BE STARTING OVER. I GET THAT.
"BUT IF WE DON'T LEAVE NOW, IF WE DON'T GO RIGHT THIS SECOND...
"...THEN EVERYTHING WILL BE OVER. FOR THEM AND US."
"I... YES... YOU'RE RIGHT."

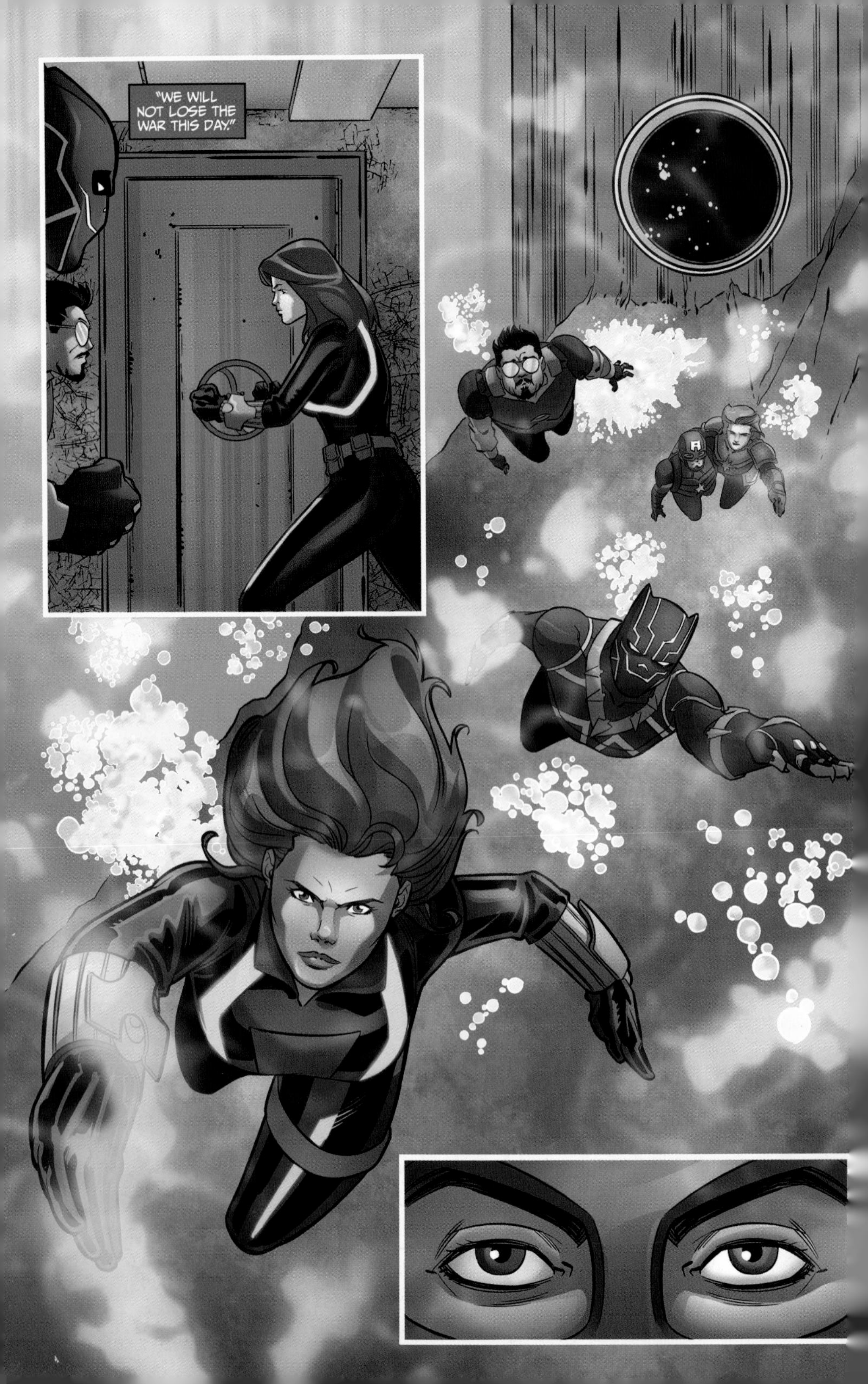
"WE WILL NOT LOSE THE WAR THIS DAY."

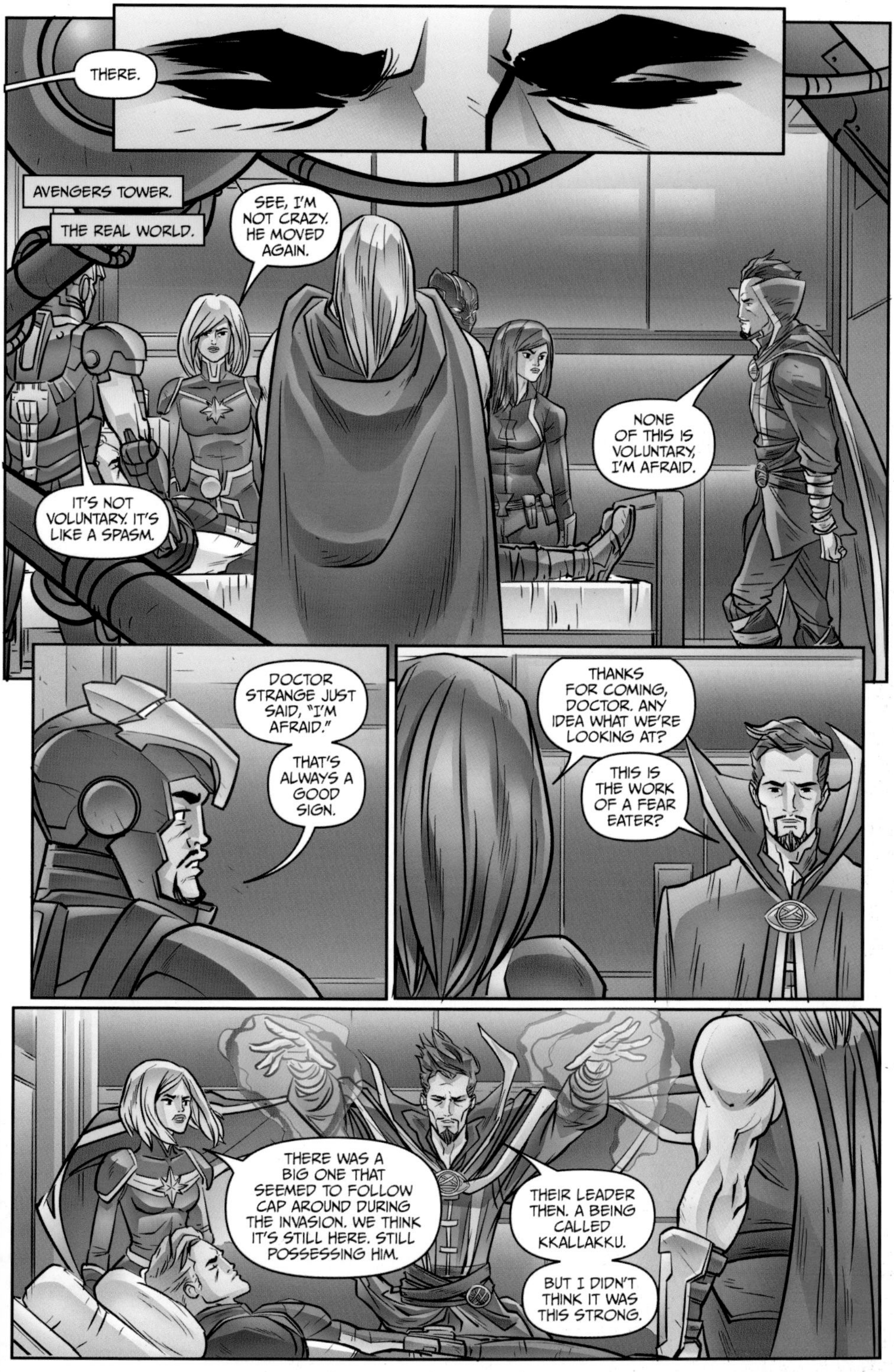
THERE.
AVENGERS TOWER.
THE REAL WORLD.
SEE, I'M NOT CRAZY. HE MOVED AGAIN.
NONE OF THIS IS VOLUNTARY, I'M AFRAID.
IT'S NOT VOLUNTARY. IT'S LIKE A SPASM.
DOCTOR STRANGE JUST SAID, "I'M AFRAID."
THAT'S ALWAYS A GOOD SIGN.
THANKS FOR COMING, DOCTOR. ANY IDEA WHAT WE'RE LOOKING AT?
THIS IS THE WORK OF A FEAR EATER?
THERE WAS A BIG ONE THAT SEEMED TO FOLLOW CAP AROUND DURING THE INVASION. WE THINK IT'S STILL HERE. STILL POSSESSING HIM.
THEIR LEADER THEN. A BEING CALLED KKALLAKKU.
BUT I DIDN'T THINK IT WAS THIS STRONG.

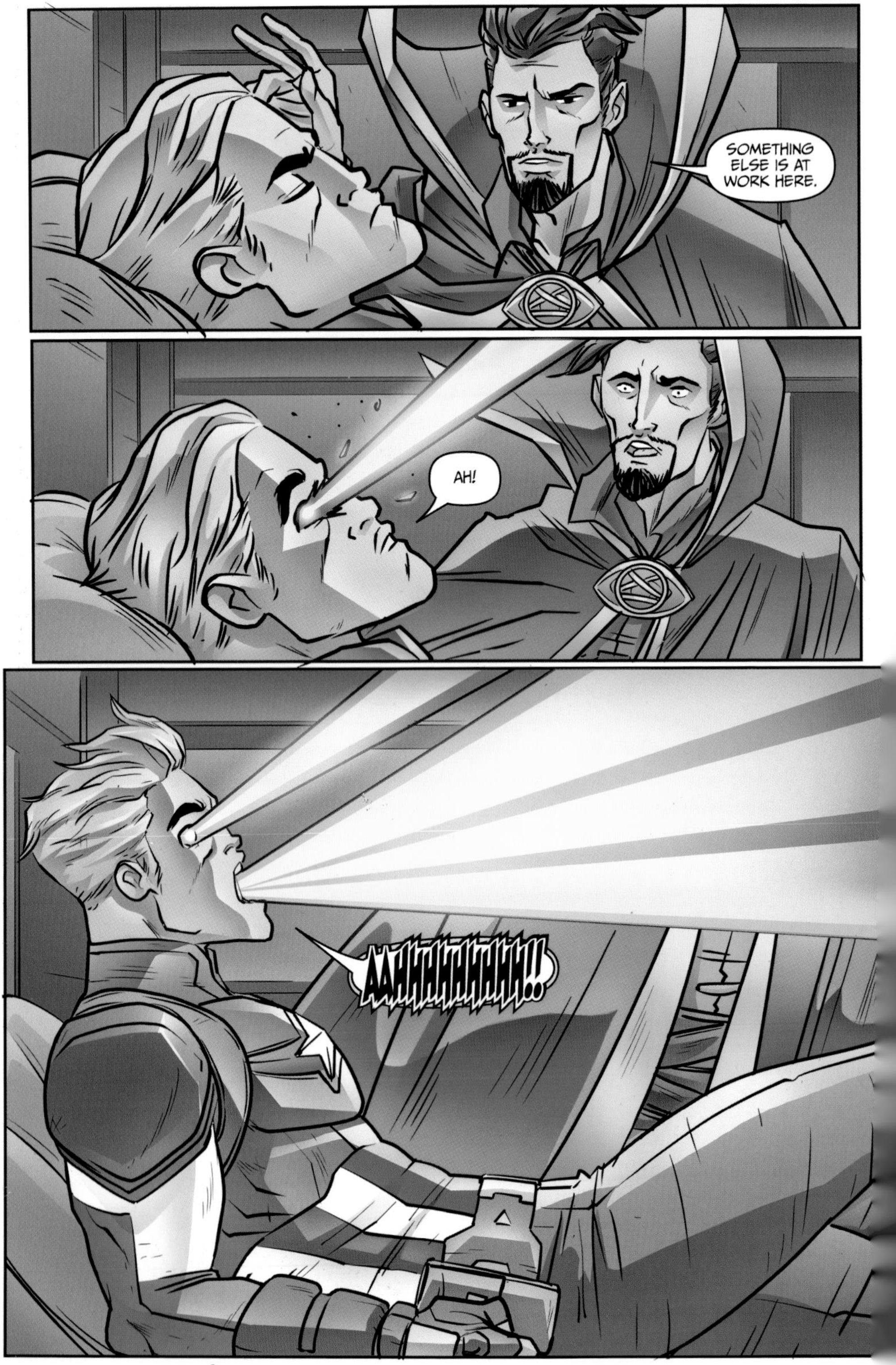
SOMETHING ELSE IS AT WORK HERE.
AH!
AAHHHHHHHHH!!

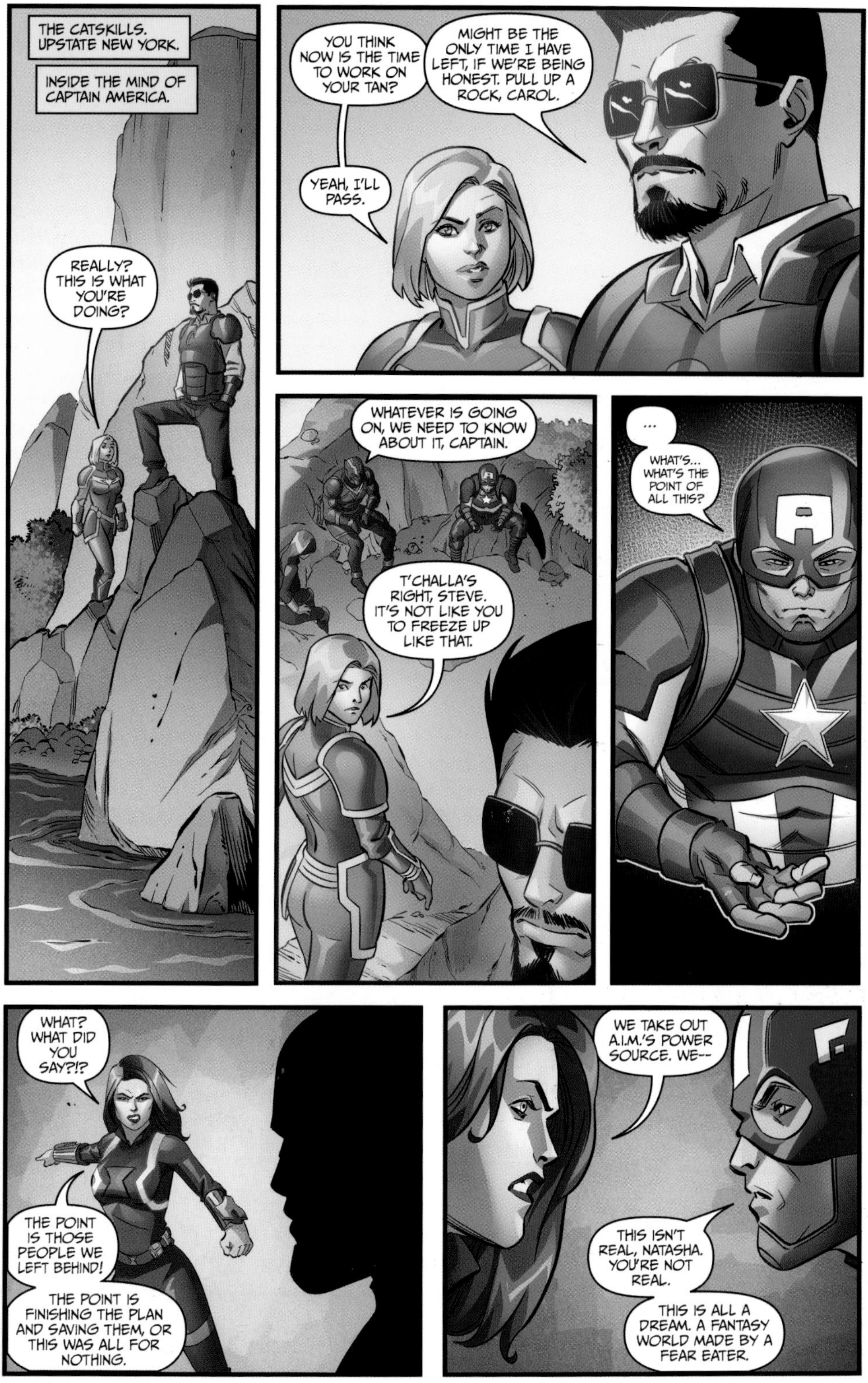
THE CATSKILLS. UPSTATE NEW YORK.
INSIDE THE MIND OF CAPTAIN AMERICA.
REALLY? THIS IS WHAT YOU'RE DOING?
YOU THINK NOW IS THE TIME TO WORK ON YOUR TAN?
MIGHT BE THE ONLY TIME I HAVE LEFT, IF WE'RE BEING HONEST. PULL UP A ROCK, CAROL.
YEAH, I'LL PASS.
WHATEVER IS GOING ON, WE NEED TO KNOW ABOUT IT, CAPTAIN.
T'CHALLA'S RIGHT, STEVE. IT'S NOT LIKE YOU TO FREEZE UP LIKE THAT.
...
WHAT'S... WHAT'S THE POINT OF ALL THIS?
WHAT? WHAT DID YOU SAY?!?
THE POINT IS THOSE PEOPLE WE LEFT BEHIND!
THE POINT IS FINISHING THE PLAN AND SAVING THEM, OR THIS WAS ALL FOR NOTHING.
WE TAKE OUT A.I.M.'S POWER SOURCE. WE--
THIS ISN'T REAL, NATASHA. YOU'RE NOT REAL.
THIS IS ALL A DREAM. A FANTASY WORLD MADE BY A FEAR EATER.

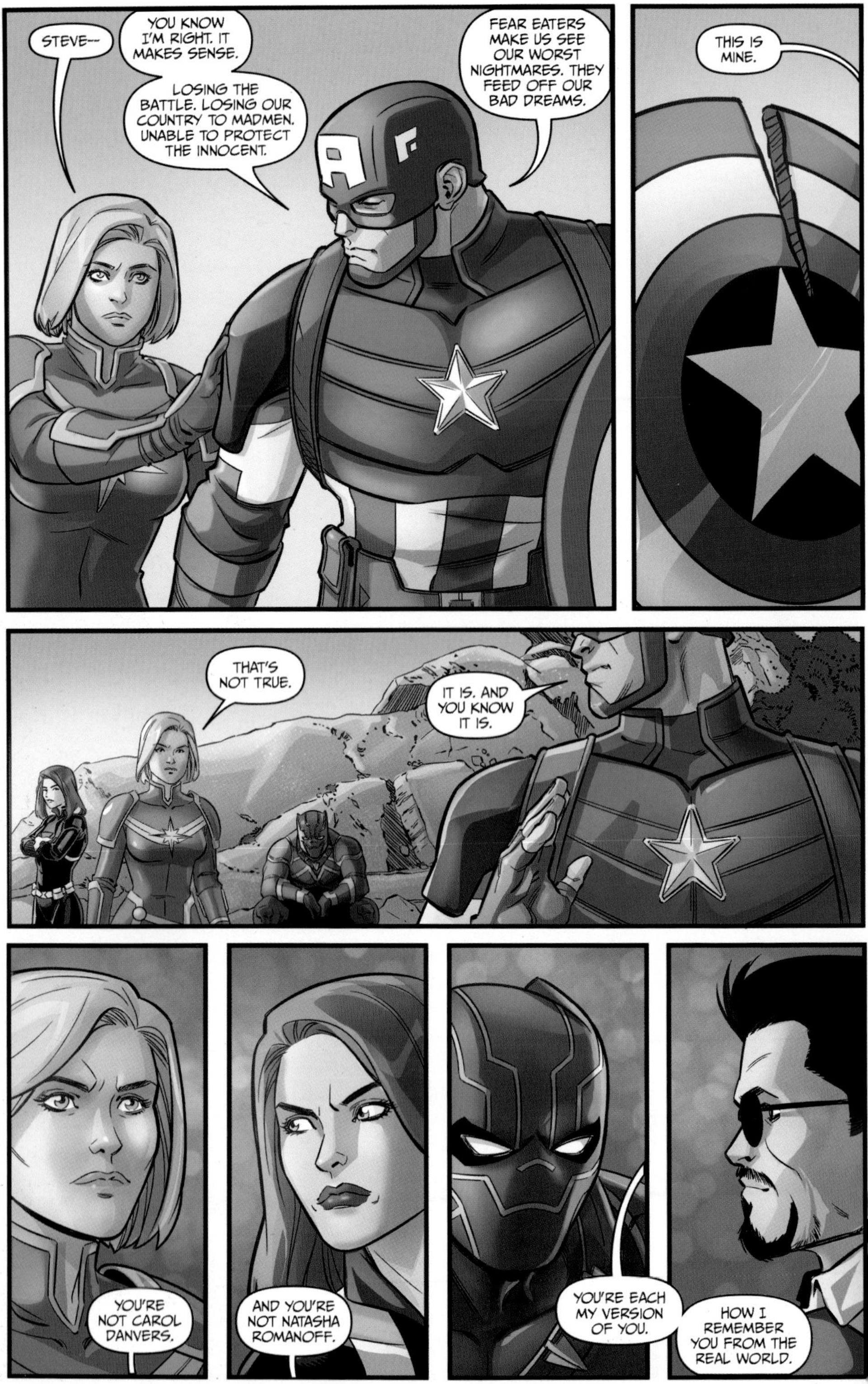
STEVE--
YOU KNOW I'M RIGHT. IT MAKES SENSE.
LOSING THE BATTLE. LOSING OUR COUNTRY TO MADMEN. UNABLE TO PROTECT THE INNOCENT.
FEAR EATERS MAKE US SEE OUR WORST NIGHTMARES. THEY FEED OFF OUR BAD DREAMS.
THIS IS MINE.
THAT'S NOT TRUE.
IT IS. AND YOU KNOW IT IS.
YOU'RE NOT CAROL DANVERS.
AND YOU'RE NOT NATASHA ROMANOFF.
YOU'RE EACH MY VERSION OF YOU.
HOW I REMEMBER YOU FROM THE REAL WORLD.

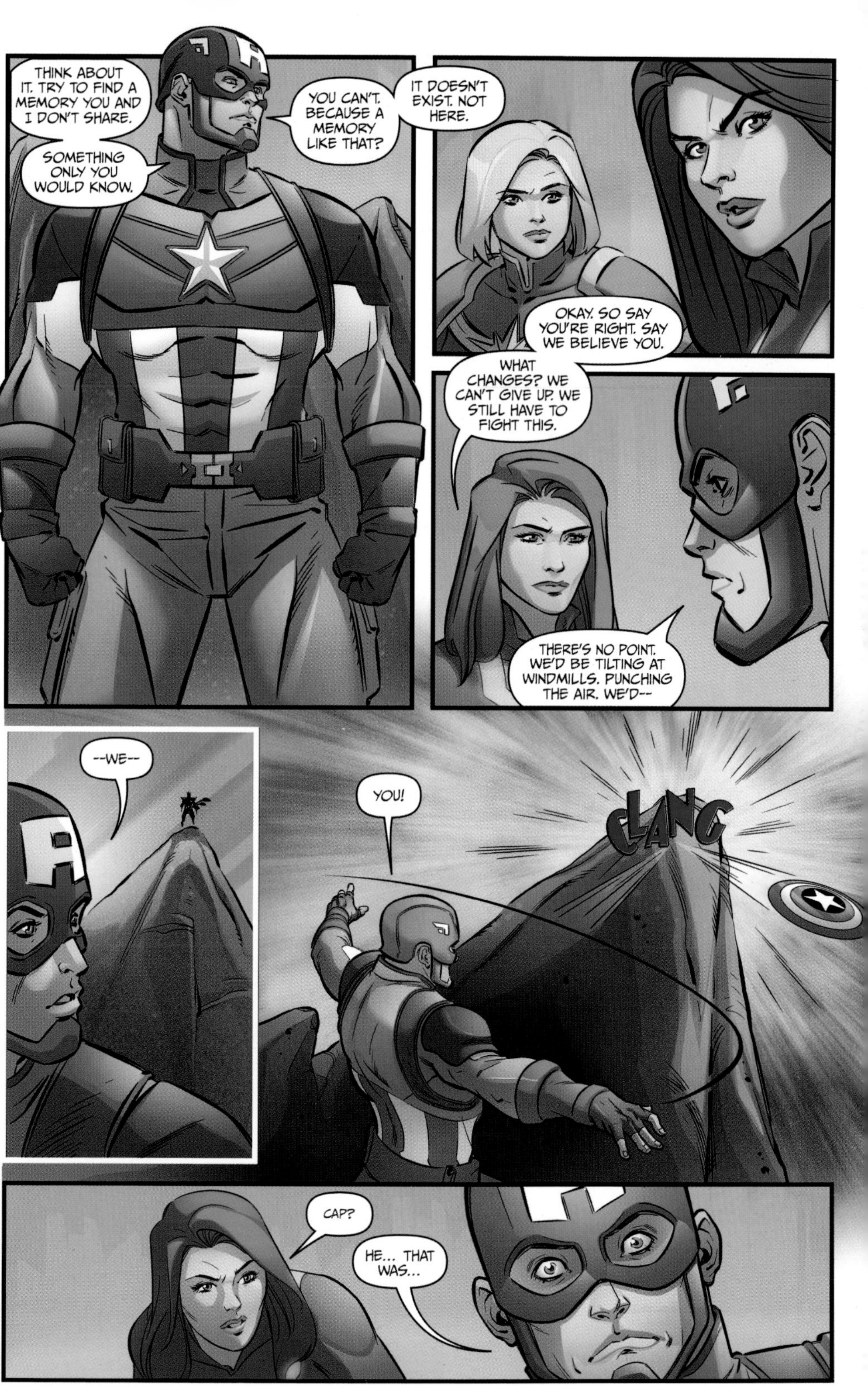
THINK ABOUT IT. TRY TO FIND A MEMORY YOU AND I DON'T SHARE.
SOMETHING ONLY YOU WOULD KNOW.
YOU CAN'T. BECAUSE A MEMORY LIKE THAT?
IT DOESN'T EXIST. NOT HERE.
OKAY. SO SAY YOU'RE RIGHT. SAY WE BELIEVE YOU.
WHAT CHANGES? WE CAN'T GIVE UP. WE STILL HAVE TO FIGHT THIS.
THERE'S NO POINT. WE'D BE TILTING AT WINDMILLS. PUNCHING THE AIR. WE'D--
--WE--
YOU!
CLANG
CAP?
HE... THAT WAS...

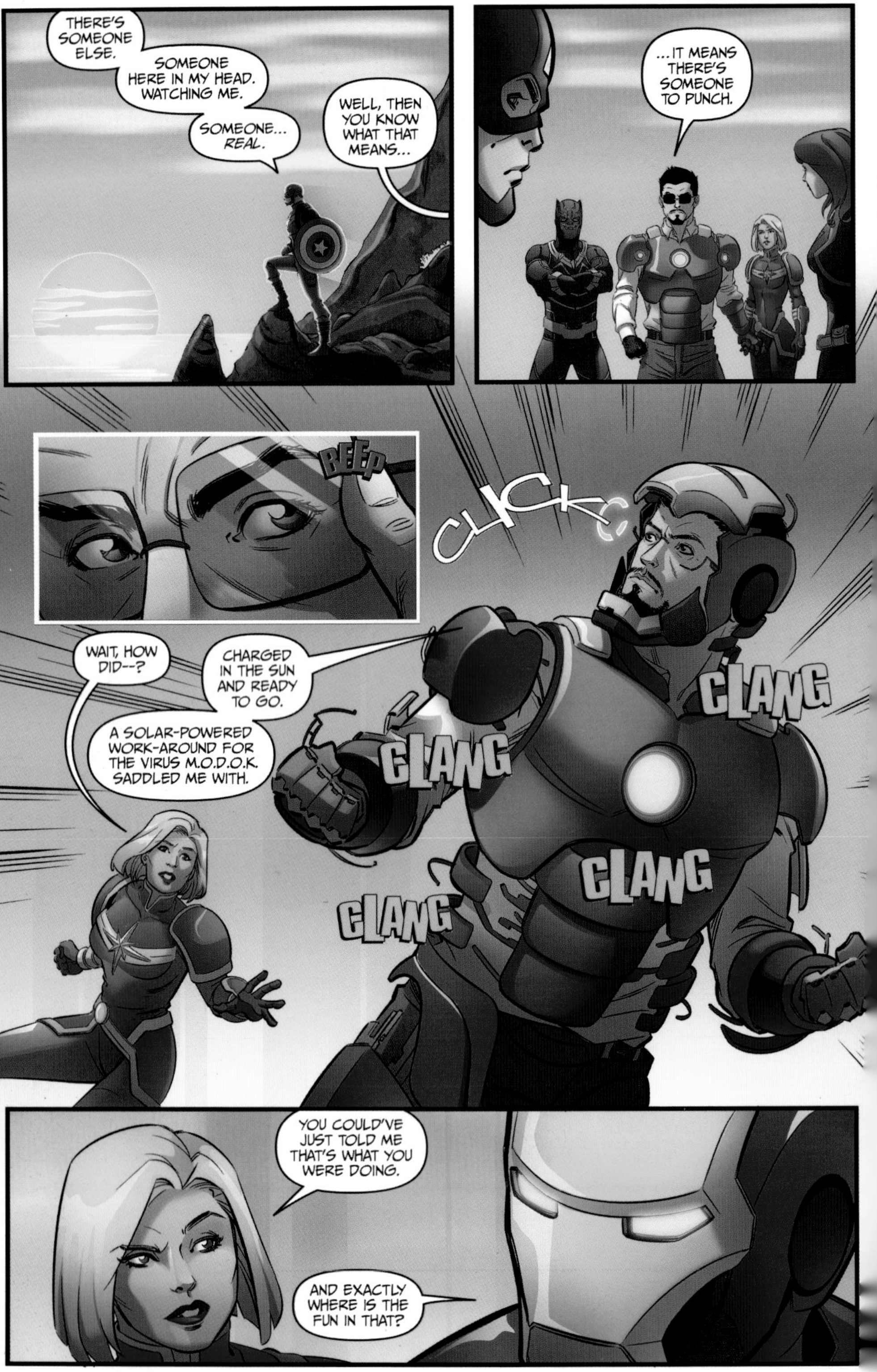
THERE'S SOMEONE ELSE.
SOMEONE HERE IN MY HEAD. WATCHING ME.
SOMEONE... *REAL.*
WELL, THEN YOU KNOW WHAT THAT MEANS...
...IT MEANS THERE'S SOMEONE TO PUNCH.
BEEP
CLICK
WAIT, HOW DID--?
CHARGED IN THE SUN AND READY TO GO.
A SOLAR-POWERED WORK-AROUND FOR THE VIRUS M.O.D.O.K. SADDLED ME WITH.
CLANG
CLANG
CLANG
CLANG
YOU COULD'VE JUST TOLD ME THAT'S WHAT YOU WERE DOING.
AND EXACTLY WHERE IS THE FUN IN THAT?

WE CAN DO THIS, CAP.

WE GO WITH WIDOW'S PLAN, AND WE TAKE THE FIGHT TO THEM.

IF YOU'RE RIGHT, AND THIS IS ALL SOME FEAR EATER HALLUCINATION, THEN WE FACE YOUR FEARS AS A TEAM.

IF WE TAKE OUT M.O.D.O.K. AND YOU'RE WRONG, THEN THAT'S ONE LESS EVIL FLOATING HEAD IN THE WORLD, AND THAT'S A-OKAY WITH ME.

TONY...

SPLISH

...

...

OKAY.

OKAY? JUST LIKE THAT?

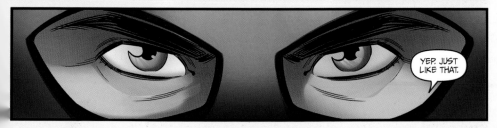

YEP. JUST LIKE THAT.

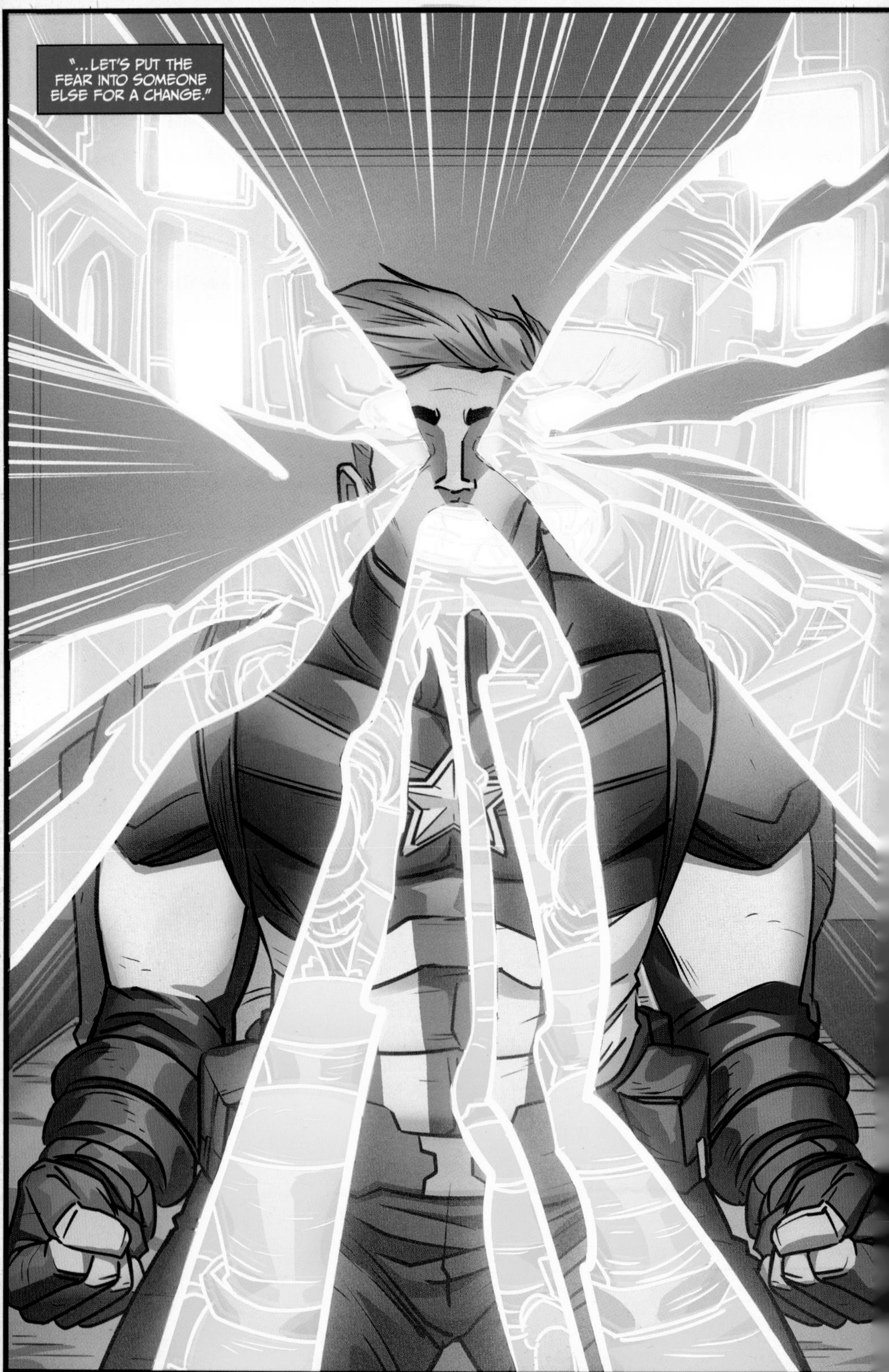
"...LET'S PUT THE FEAR INTO SOMEONE ELSE FOR A CHANGE."

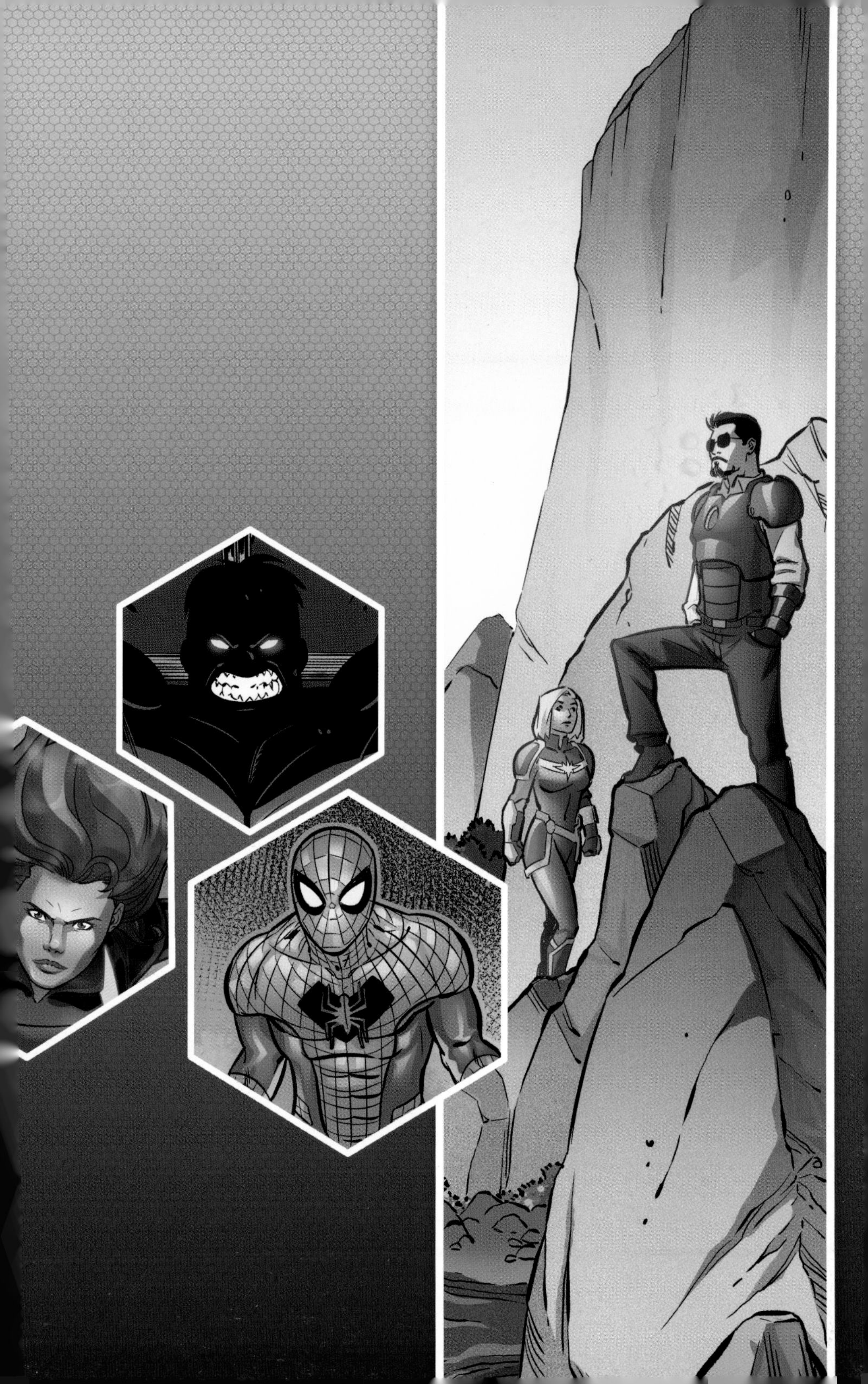

ART BY: JON SOMMARIVA
COLORS BY: PAC23

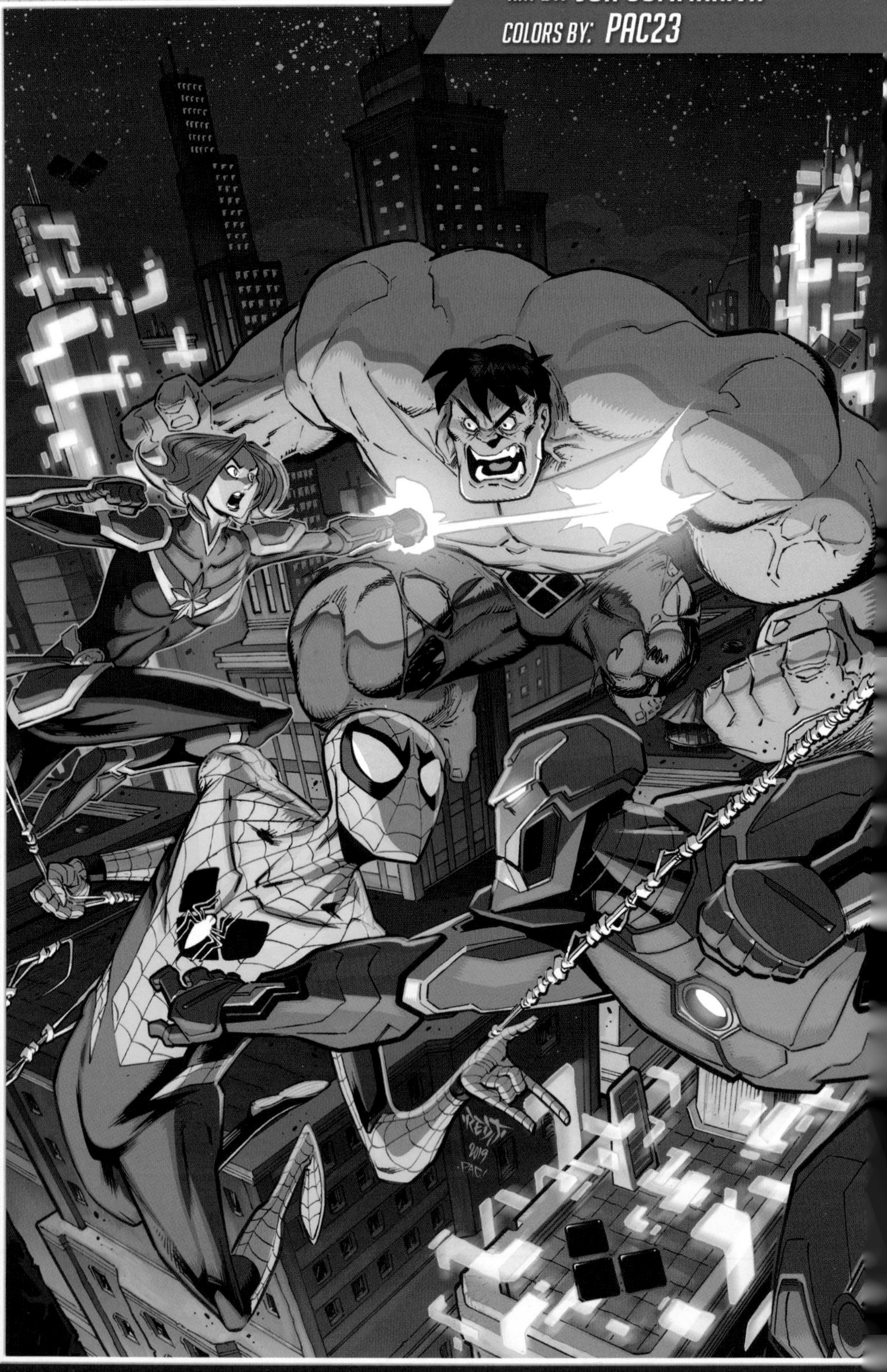

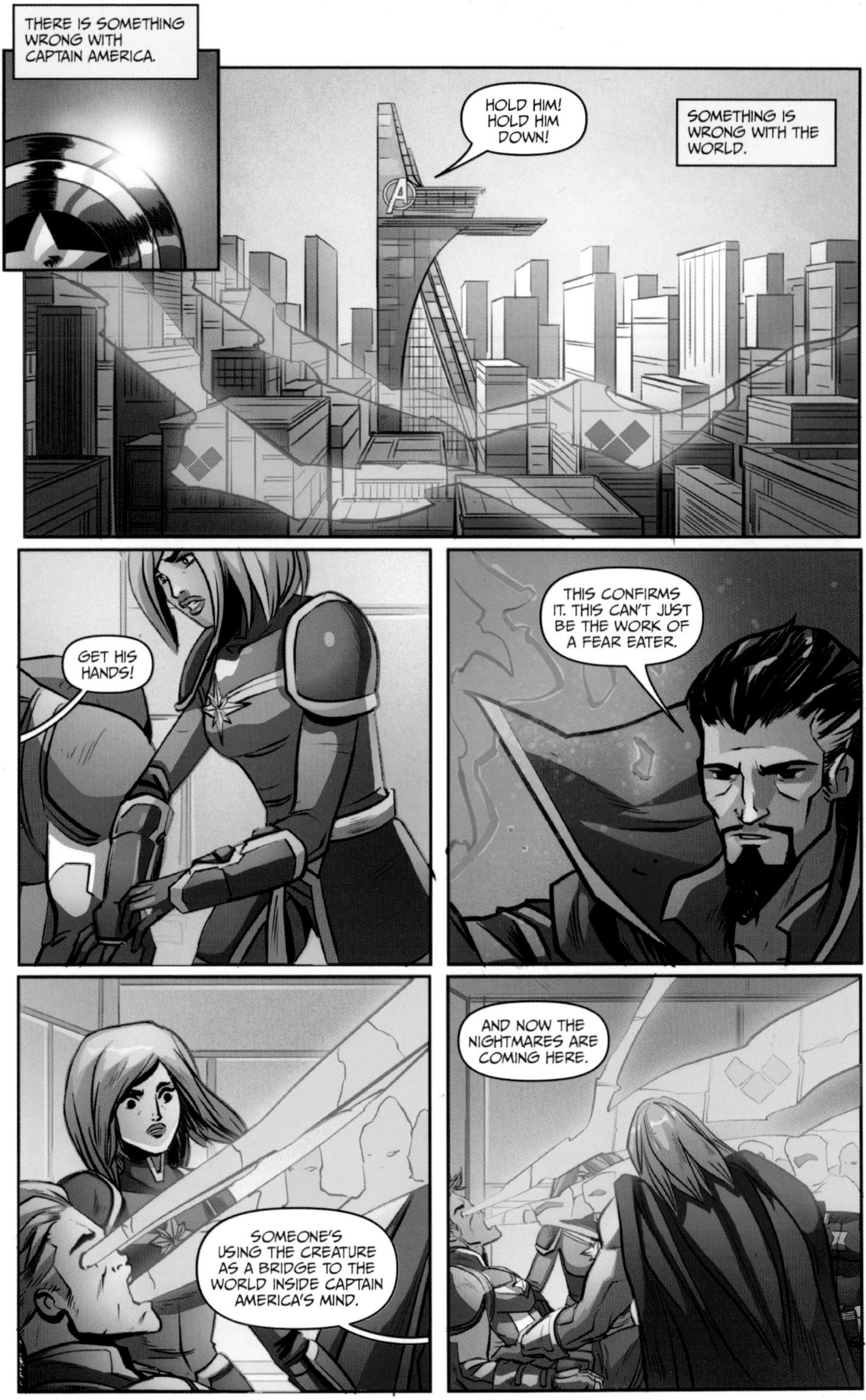
THERE IS SOMETHING WRONG WITH CAPTAIN AMERICA.
HOLD HIM! HOLD HIM DOWN!
SOMETHING IS WRONG WITH THE WORLD.
GET HIS HANDS!
THIS CONFIRMS IT. THIS CAN'T JUST BE THE WORK OF A FEAR EATER.
SOMEONE'S USING THE CREATURE AS A BRIDGE TO THE WORLD INSIDE CAPTAIN AMERICA'S MIND.
AND NOW THE NIGHTMARES ARE COMING HERE.

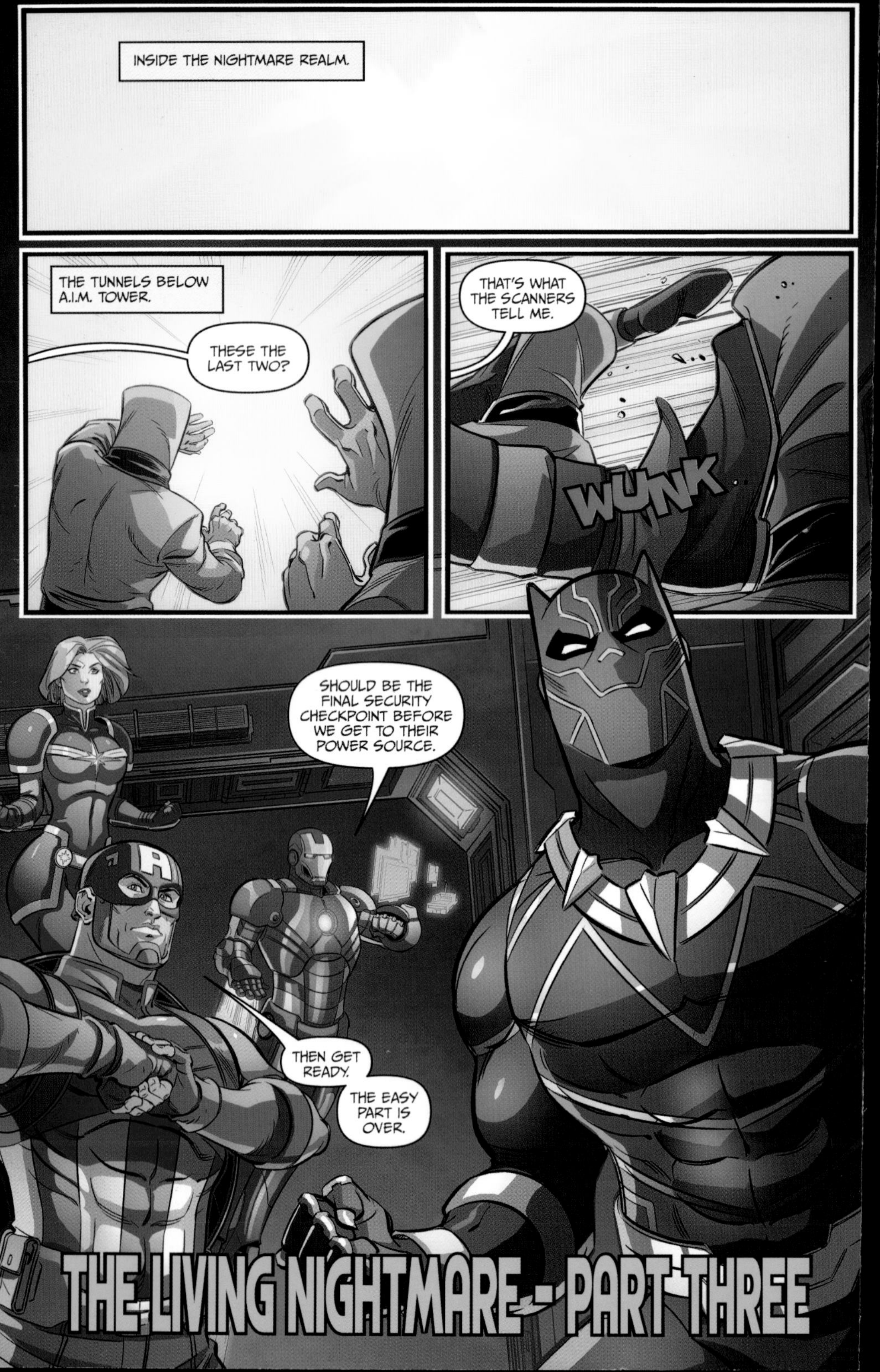
INSIDE THE NIGHTMARE REALM.
THE TUNNELS BELOW A.I.M. TOWER.
THESE THE LAST TWO?
THAT'S WHAT THE SCANNERS TELL ME.
WUNK
SHOULD BE THE FINAL SECURITY CHECKPOINT BEFORE WE GET TO THEIR POWER SOURCE.
THEN GET READY.
THE EASY PART IS OVER.
THE LIVING NIGHTMARE - PART THREE

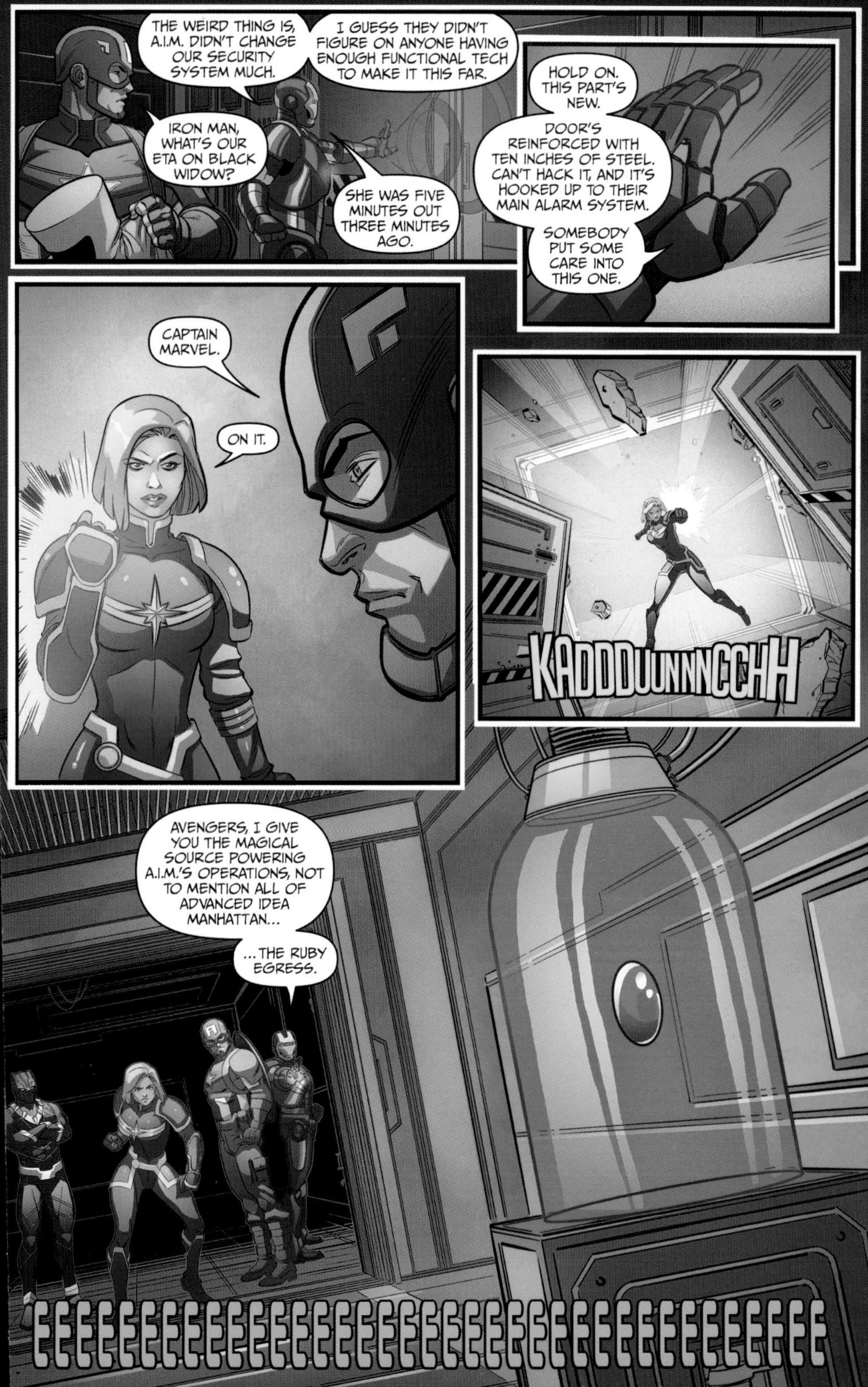
THE WEIRD THING IS, A.I.M. DIDN'T CHANGE OUR SECURITY SYSTEM MUCH.
I GUESS THEY DIDN'T FIGURE ON ANYONE HAVING ENOUGH FUNCTIONAL TECH TO MAKE IT THIS FAR.
IRON MAN, WHAT'S OUR ETA ON BLACK WIDOW?
SHE WAS FIVE MINUTES OUT THREE MINUTES AGO.
HOLD ON. THIS PART'S NEW.
DOOR'S REINFORCED WITH TEN INCHES OF STEEL. CAN'T HACK IT, AND IT'S HOOKED UP TO THEIR MAIN ALARM SYSTEM.
SOMEBODY PUT SOME CARE INTO THIS ONE.
CAPTAIN MARVEL.
ON IT.
KADDDUUNNNCCHH
AVENGERS, I GIVE YOU THE MAGICAL SOURCE POWERING A.I.M.'S OPERATIONS, NOT TO MENTION ALL OF ADVANCED IDEA MANHATTAN...
...THE RUBY EGRESS.
EEEEEEEEEEEEEEEEEEEEEEEEEEEEEEEEEEEEEEE

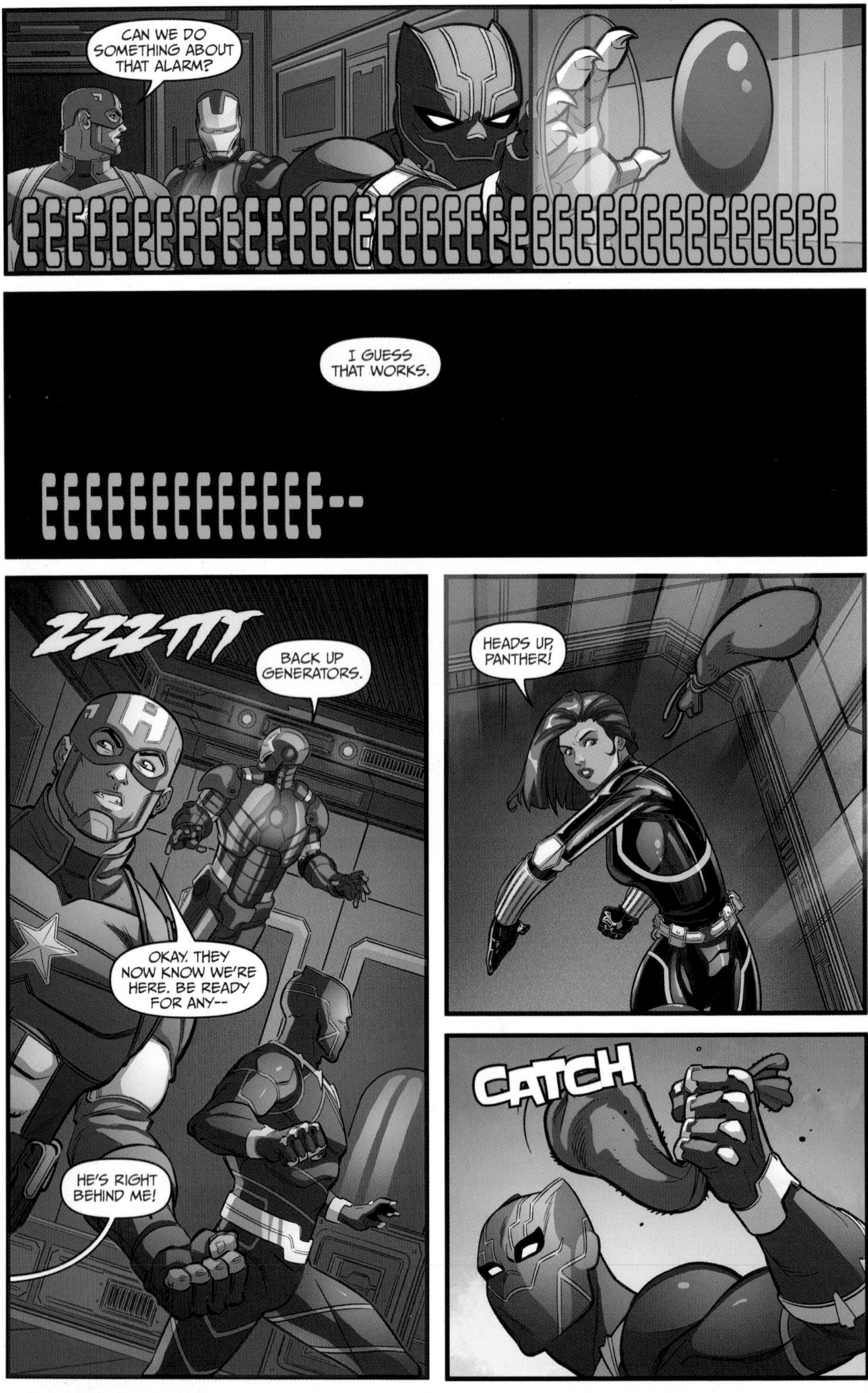
CAN WE DO SOMETHING ABOUT THAT ALARM?
EEEEEEEEEEEEEEEEEEEEEEEEEEEEEEEEEEEEEEEE
I GUESS THAT WORKS.
EEEEEEEEEEEEE--
ZZZTTT
BACK UP GENERATORS.
OKAY. THEY NOW KNOW WE'RE HERE. BE READY FOR ANY--
HE'S RIGHT BEHIND ME!
HEADS UP, PANTHER!
CATCH

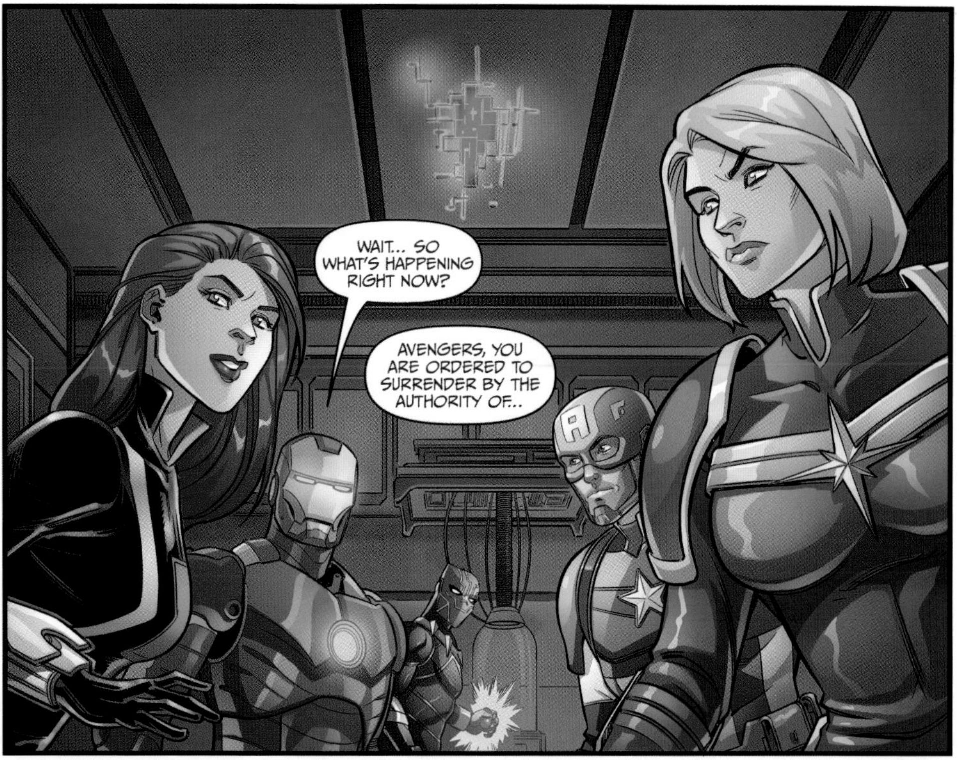
WAIT... SO WHAT'S HAPPENING RIGHT NOW?
AVENGERS, YOU ARE ORDERED TO SURRENDER BY THE AUTHORITY OF...

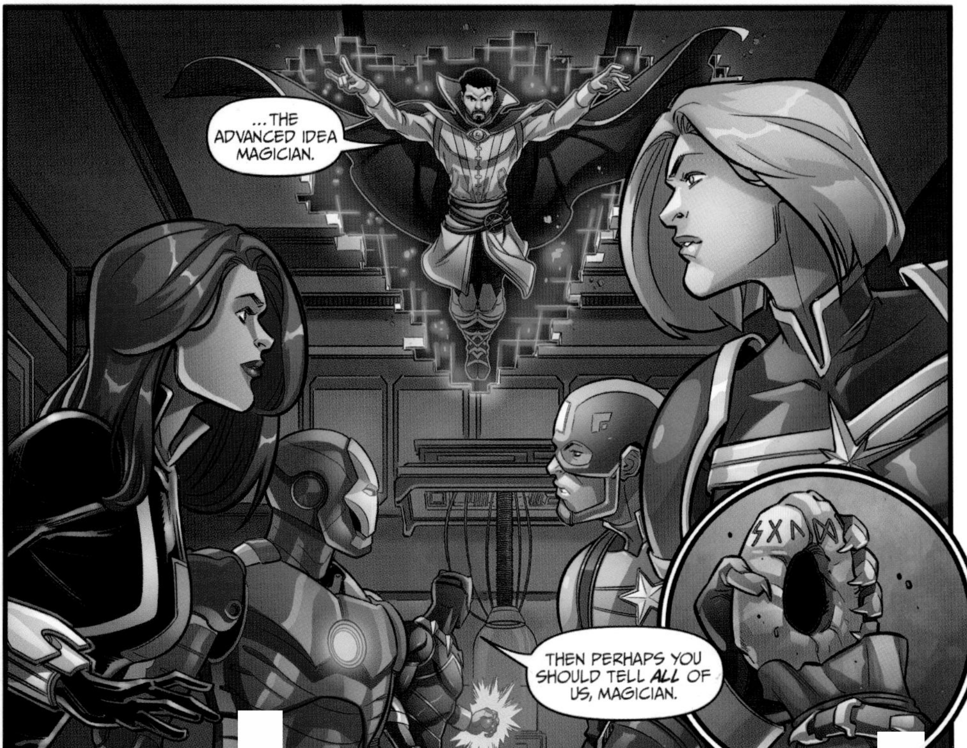
...THE ADVANCED IDEA MAGICIAN.
THEN PERHAPS YOU SHOULD TELL ***ALL*** OF US, MAGICIAN.

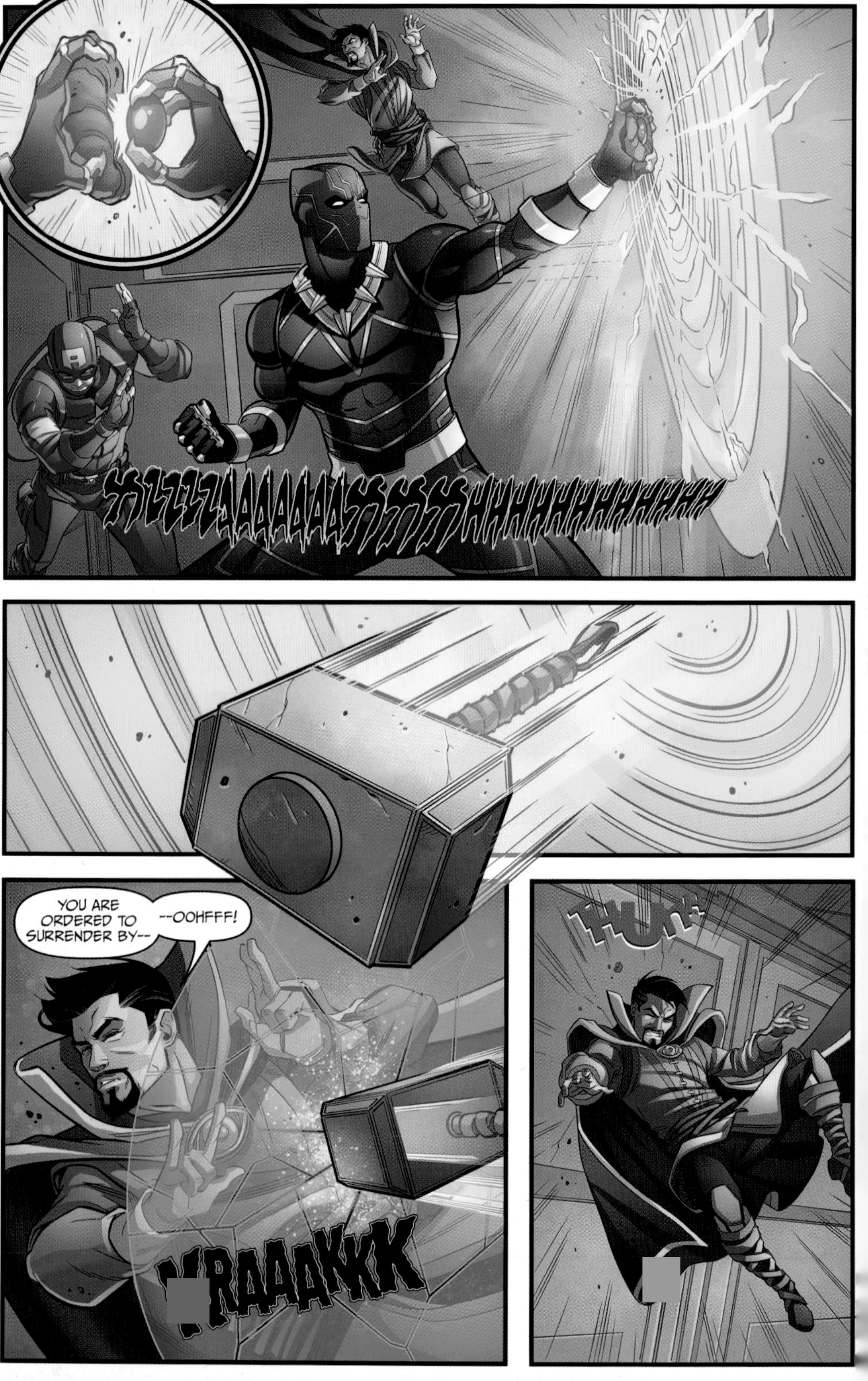
SSZZZZAAAAAAASSSSSHHHHHHHHHHH
YOU ARE ORDERED TO SURRENDER BY--
--OOHFFF!
RAAAKK
THUNK

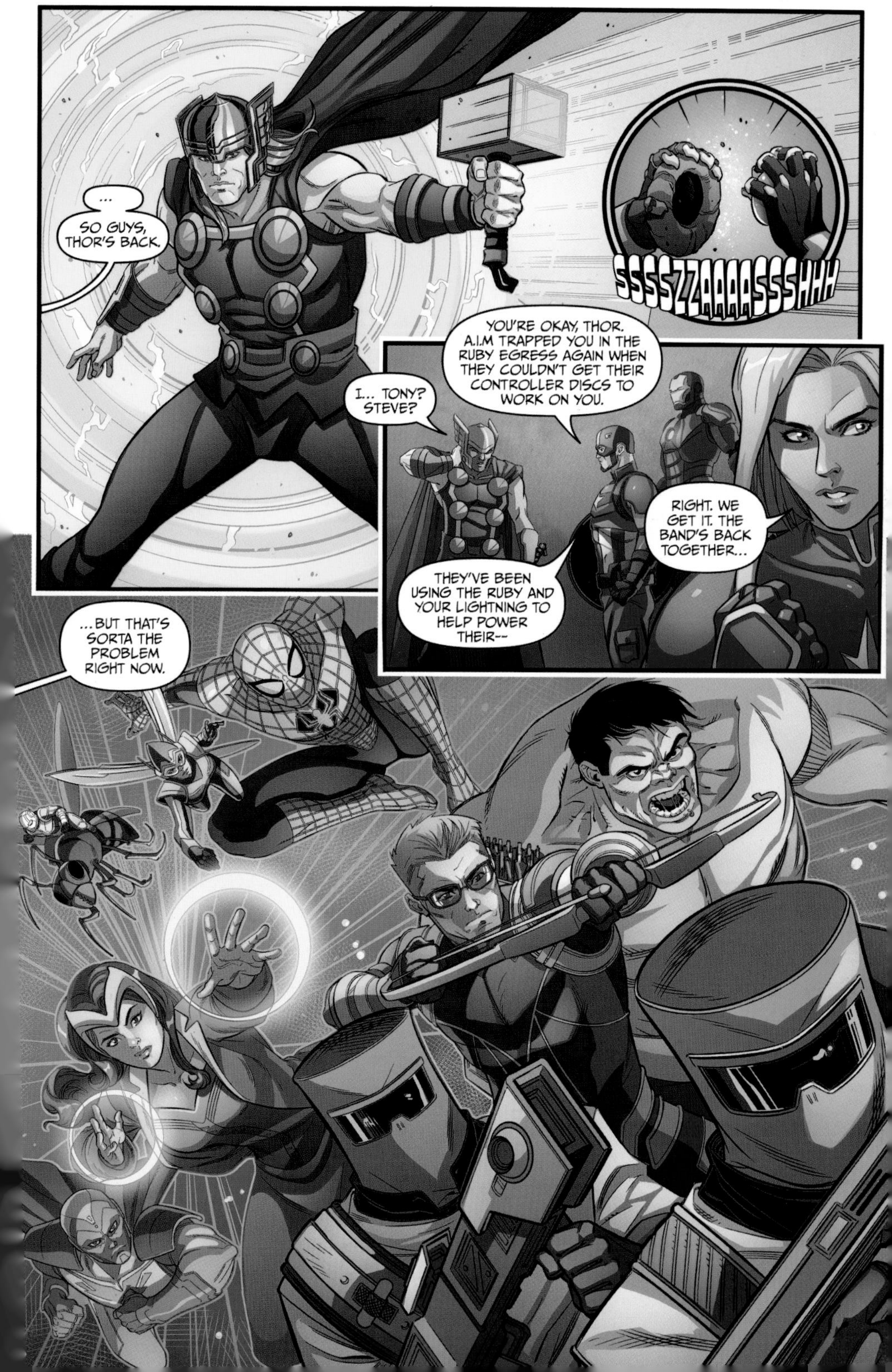
...
SO GUYS, THOR'S BACK.
SSSSZZAAAASSSHHH
I... TONY? STEVE?
YOU'RE OKAY, THOR. A.I.M TRAPPED YOU IN THE RUBY EGRESS AGAIN WHEN THEY COULDN'T GET THEIR CONTROLLER DISCS TO WORK ON YOU.
THEY'VE BEEN USING THE RUBY AND YOUR LIGHTNING TO HELP POWER THEIR--
RIGHT. WE GET IT. THE BAND'S BACK TOGETHER...
...BUT THAT'S SORTA THE PROBLEM RIGHT NOW.

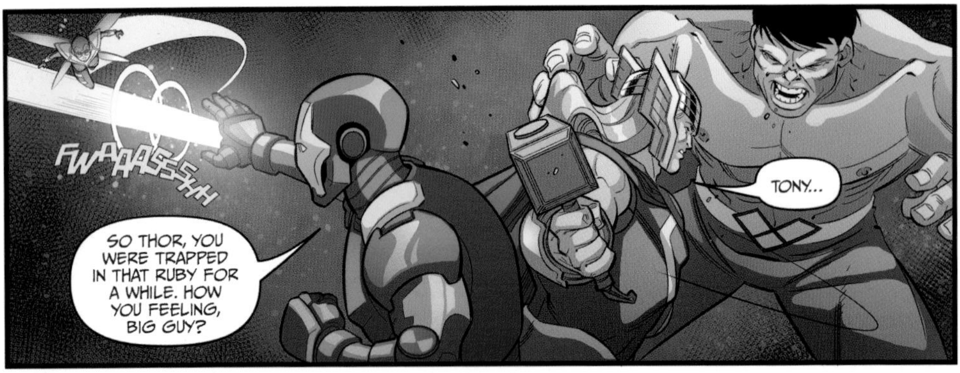
FWAAASSSHH
SO THOR, YOU WERE TRAPPED IN THAT RUBY FOR A WHILE. HOW YOU FEELING, BIG GUY?
TONY...

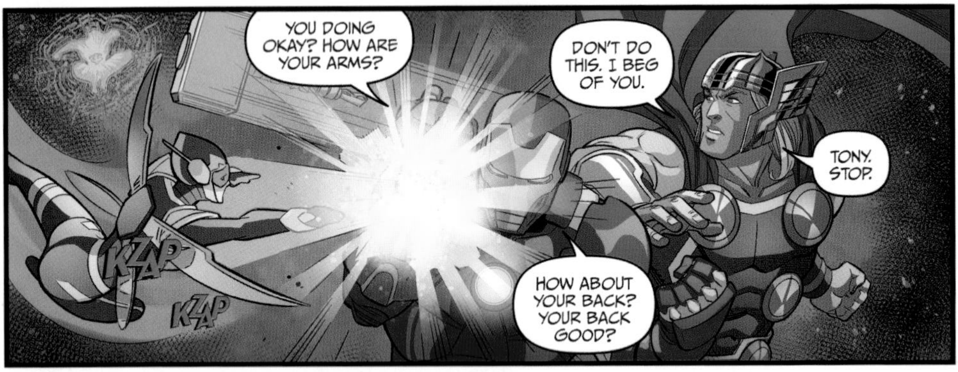
YOU DOING OKAY? HOW ARE YOUR ARMS?
DON'T DO THIS. I BEG OF YOU.
TONY. STOP.
KZAP
KZAP
HOW ABOUT YOUR BACK? YOUR BACK GOOD?

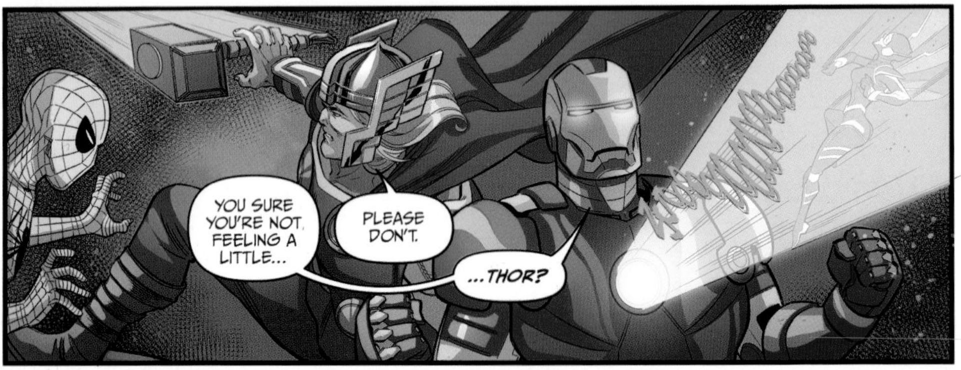
YOU SURE YOU'RE NOT FEELING A LITTLE...
PLEASE DON'T.
...THOR?

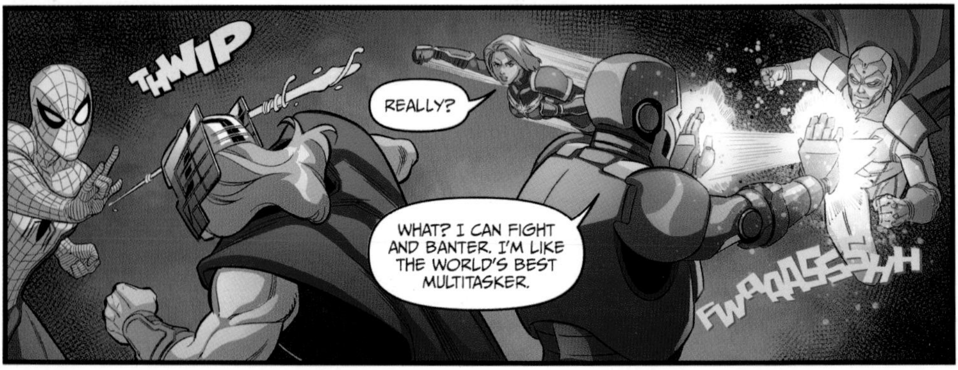
THWIP
REALLY?
WHAT? I CAN FIGHT AND BANTER. I'M LIKE THE WORLD'S BEST MULTITASKER.
FWAAASSSHH

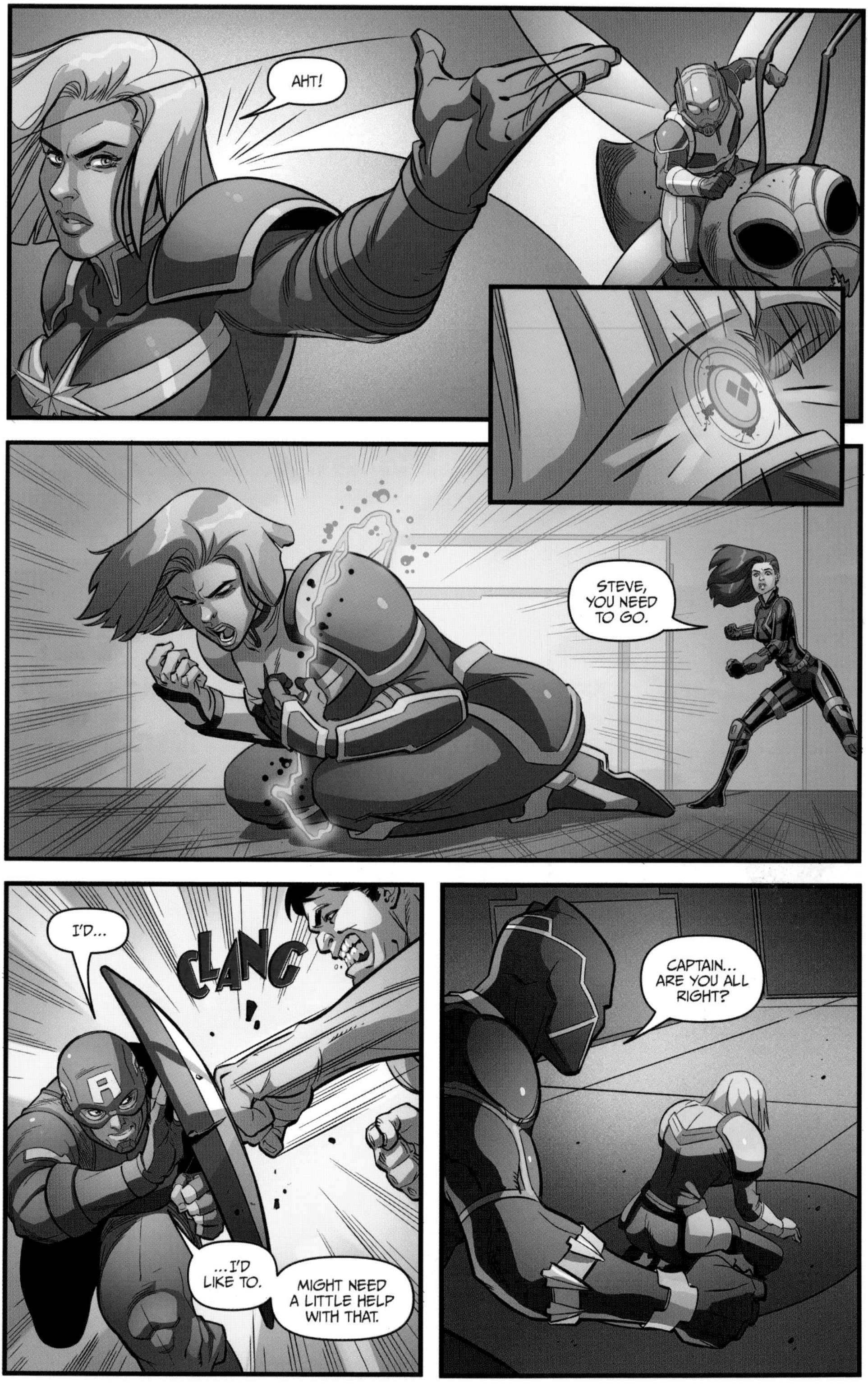
AHT!
STEVE, YOU NEED TO GO.
I'D...
CLANG
...I'D LIKE TO.
MIGHT NEED A LITTLE HELP WITH THAT.
CAPTAIN... ARE YOU ALL RIGHT?

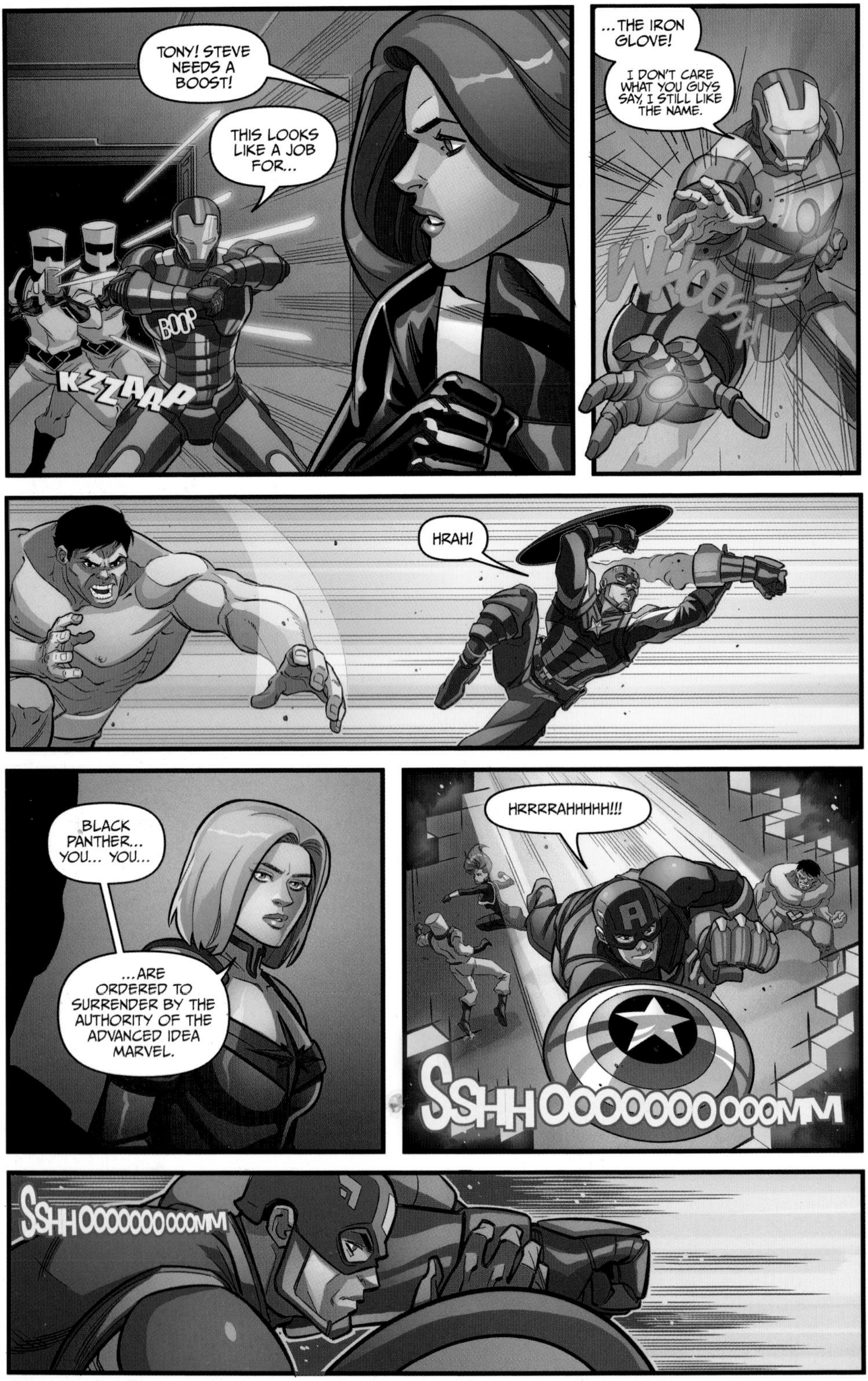
TONY! STEVE NEEDS A BOOST!
THIS LOOKS LIKE A JOB FOR...
BOOP
KZZAAP
...THE IRON GLOVE!
I DON'T CARE WHAT YOU GUYS SAY, I STILL LIKE THE NAME.
WHOOSH
HRAH!
BLACK PANTHER... YOU... YOU...
...ARE ORDERED TO SURRENDER BY THE AUTHORITY OF THE ADVANCED IDEA MARVEL.
HRRRRAHHHHH!!!
SSHHOOOOOOOOOOMM
SSHHOOOOOOOOOOMM

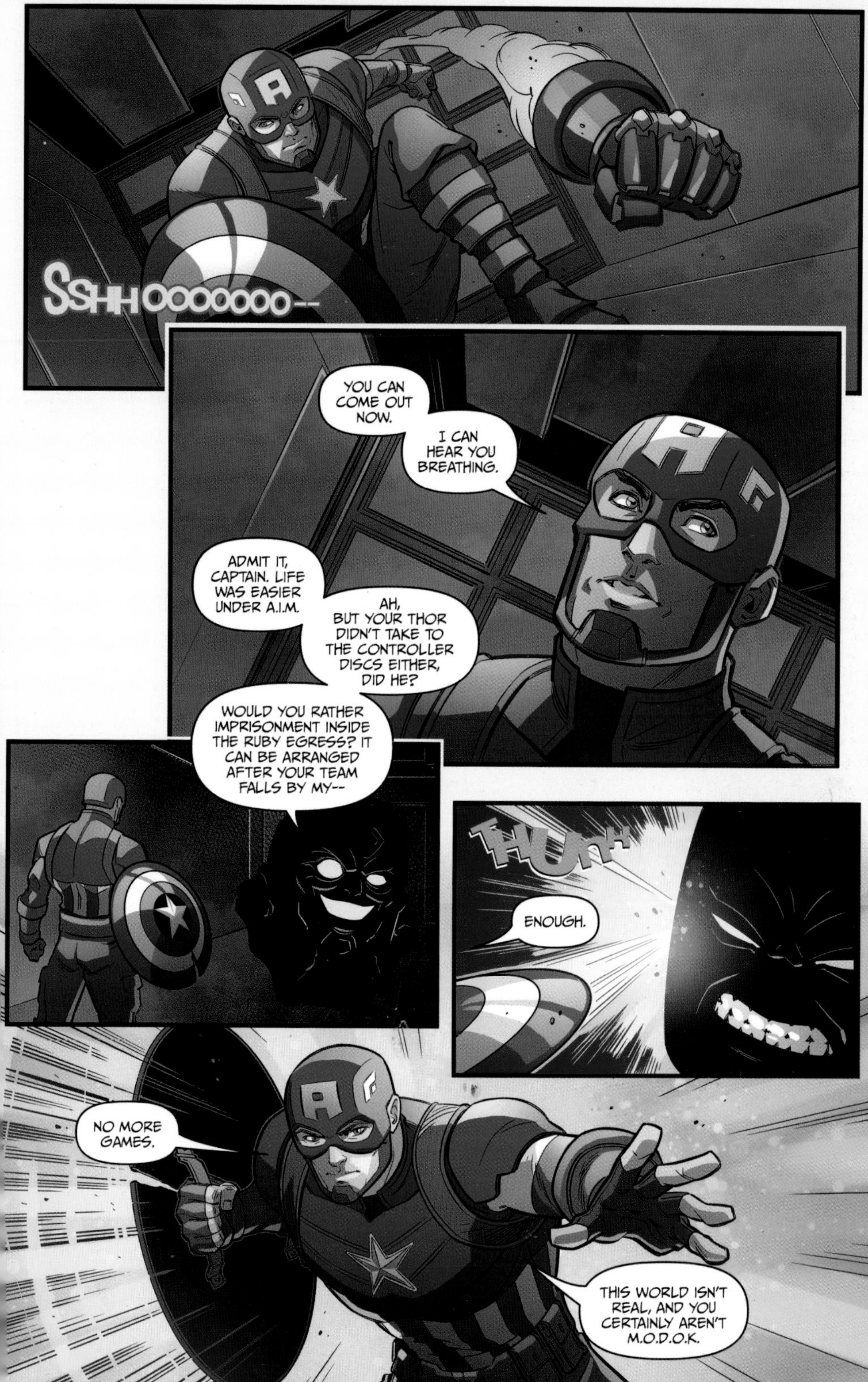
SSHHOOOOOOO--
YOU CAN COME OUT NOW.
I CAN HEAR YOU BREATHING.
ADMIT IT, CAPTAIN. LIFE WAS EASIER UNDER A.I.M.
AH, BUT YOUR THOR DIDN'T TAKE TO THE CONTROLLER DISCS EITHER, DID HE?
WOULD YOU RATHER IMPRISONMENT INSIDE THE RUBY EGRESS? IT CAN BE ARRANGED AFTER YOUR TEAM FALLS BY MY--
THUNK
ENOUGH.
NO MORE GAMES.
THIS WORLD ISN'T REAL, AND YOU CERTAINLY AREN'T M.O.D.O.K.

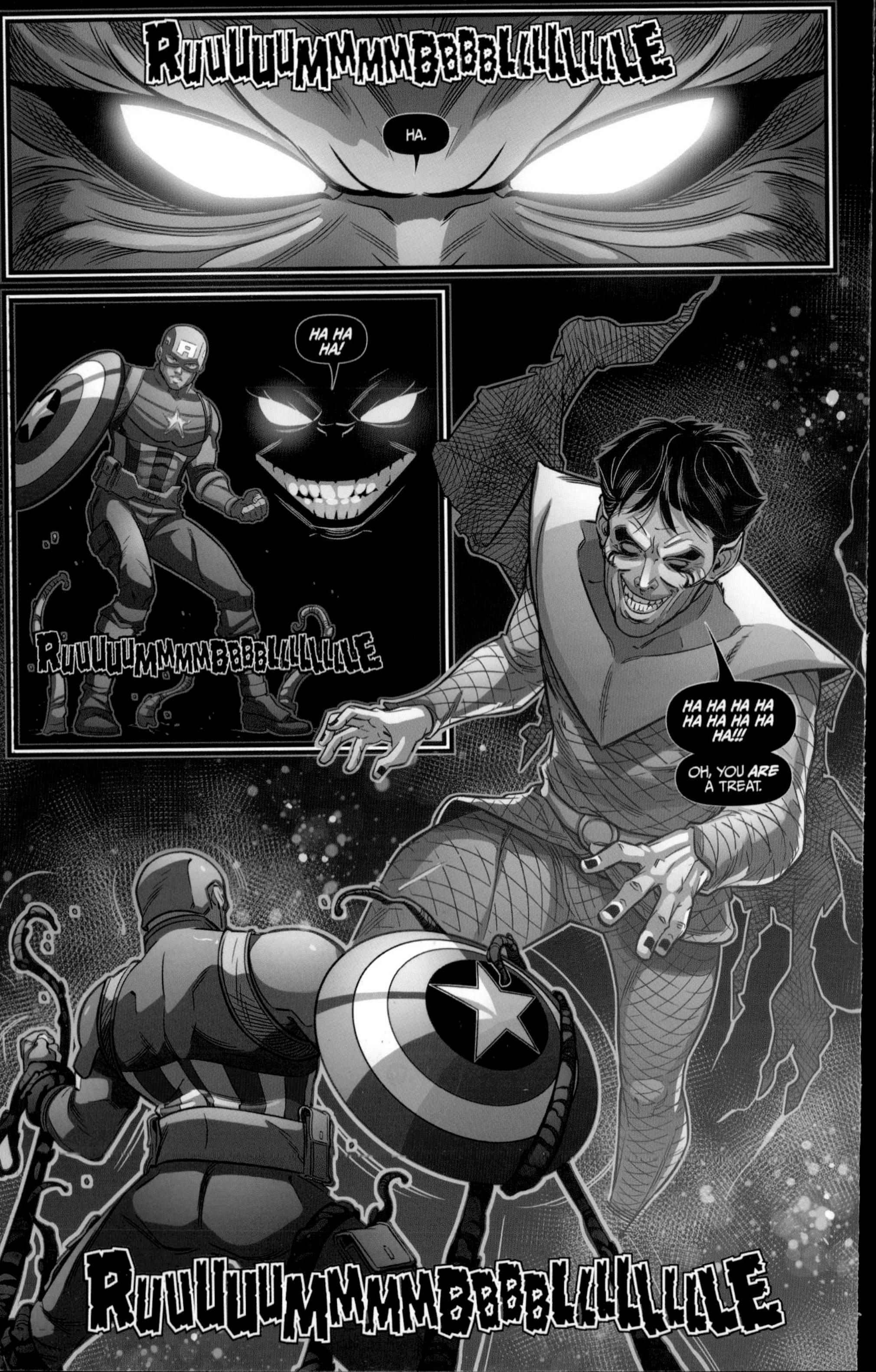
RUUUUUMMMMBBBBLLLLLLLLE
HA.
HA HA HA!
RUUUUUMMMMBBBBLLLLLLLLE
HA HA HA HA HA HA HA HA HA!!!
OH, YOU *ARE* A TREAT.
RUUUUUMMMMBBBBLLLLLLLLE

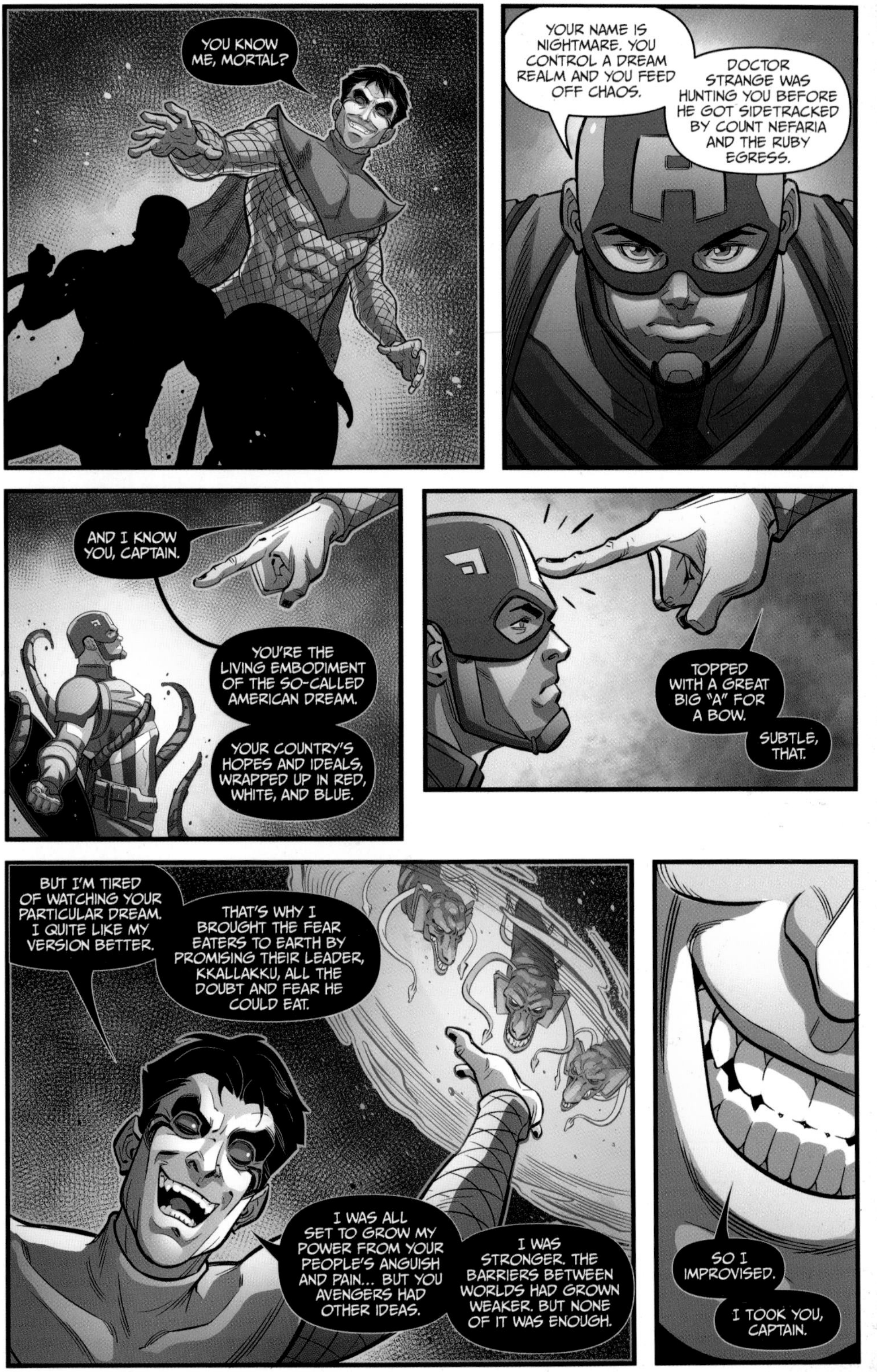
YOU KNOW ME, MORTAL?
YOUR NAME IS NIGHTMARE. YOU CONTROL A DREAM REALM AND YOU FEED OFF CHAOS.
DOCTOR STRANGE WAS HUNTING YOU BEFORE HE GOT SIDETRACKED BY COUNT NEFARIA AND THE RUBY EGRESS.
AND I KNOW YOU, CAPTAIN.
YOU'RE THE LIVING EMBODIMENT OF THE SO-CALLED AMERICAN DREAM.
YOUR COUNTRY'S HOPES AND IDEALS, WRAPPED UP IN RED, WHITE, AND BLUE.
TOPPED WITH A GREAT BIG "A" FOR A BOW.
SUBTLE, THAT.
BUT I'M TIRED OF WATCHING YOUR PARTICULAR DREAM. I QUITE LIKE MY VERSION BETTER.
THAT'S WHY I BROUGHT THE FEAR EATERS TO EARTH BY PROMISING THEIR LEADER, KKALLAKKU, ALL THE DOUBT AND FEAR HE COULD EAT.
I WAS ALL SET TO GROW MY POWER FROM YOUR PEOPLE'S ANGUISH AND PAIN... BUT YOU AVENGERS HAD OTHER IDEAS.
I WAS STRONGER. THE BARRIERS BETWEEN WORLDS HAD GROWN WEAKER. BUT NONE OF IT WAS ENOUGH.
SO I IMPROVISED.
I TOOK YOU, CAPTAIN.

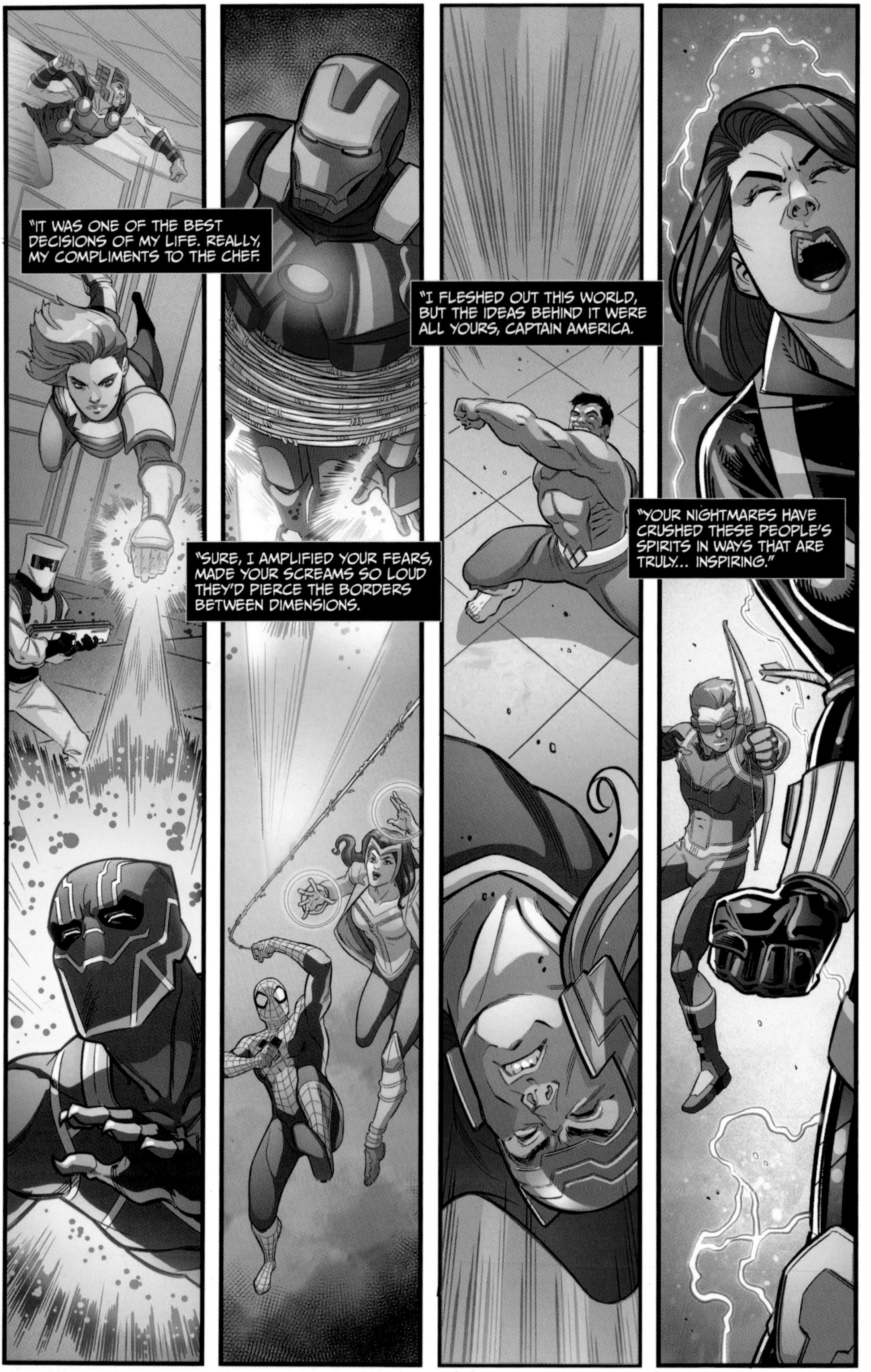
"IT WAS ONE OF THE BEST DECISIONS OF MY LIFE. REALLY, MY COMPLIMENTS TO THE CHEF.
"SURE, I AMPLIFIED YOUR FEARS, MADE YOUR SCREAMS SO LOUD THEY'D PIERCE THE BORDERS BETWEEN DIMENSIONS.
"I FLESHED OUT THIS WORLD, BUT THE IDEAS BEHIND IT WERE ALL YOURS, CAPTAIN AMERICA.
"YOUR NIGHTMARES HAVE CRUSHED THESE PEOPLE'S SPIRITS IN WAYS THAT ARE TRULY... INSPIRING."

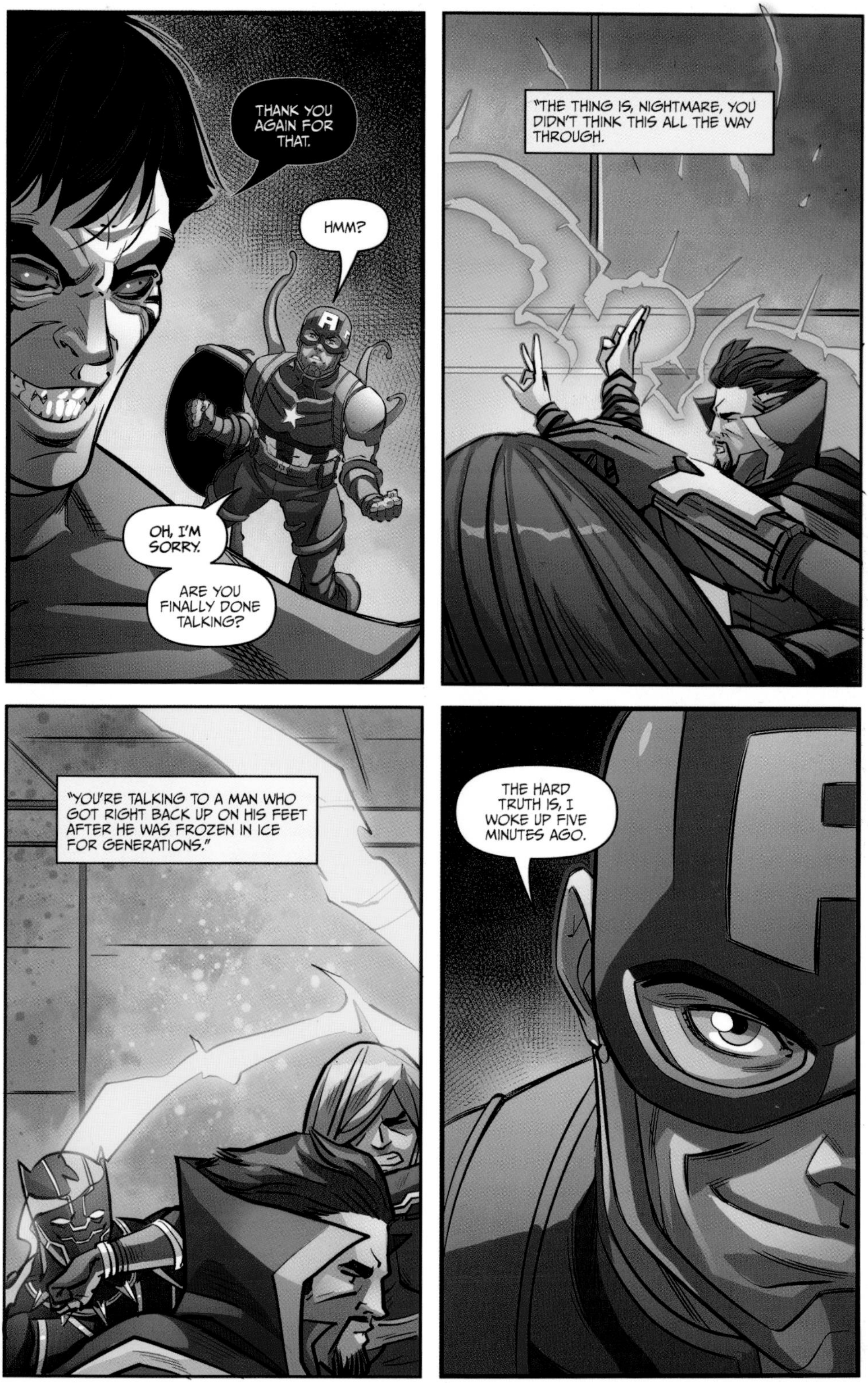

THANK YOU AGAIN FOR THAT.
HMM?
OH, I'M SORRY.
ARE YOU FINALLY DONE TALKING?
"THE THING IS, NIGHTMARE, YOU DIDN'T THINK THIS ALL THE WAY THROUGH.
"YOU'RE TALKING TO A MAN WHO GOT RIGHT BACK UP ON HIS FEET AFTER HE WAS FROZEN IN ICE FOR GENERATIONS."
THE HARD TRUTH IS, I WOKE UP FIVE MINUTES AGO.

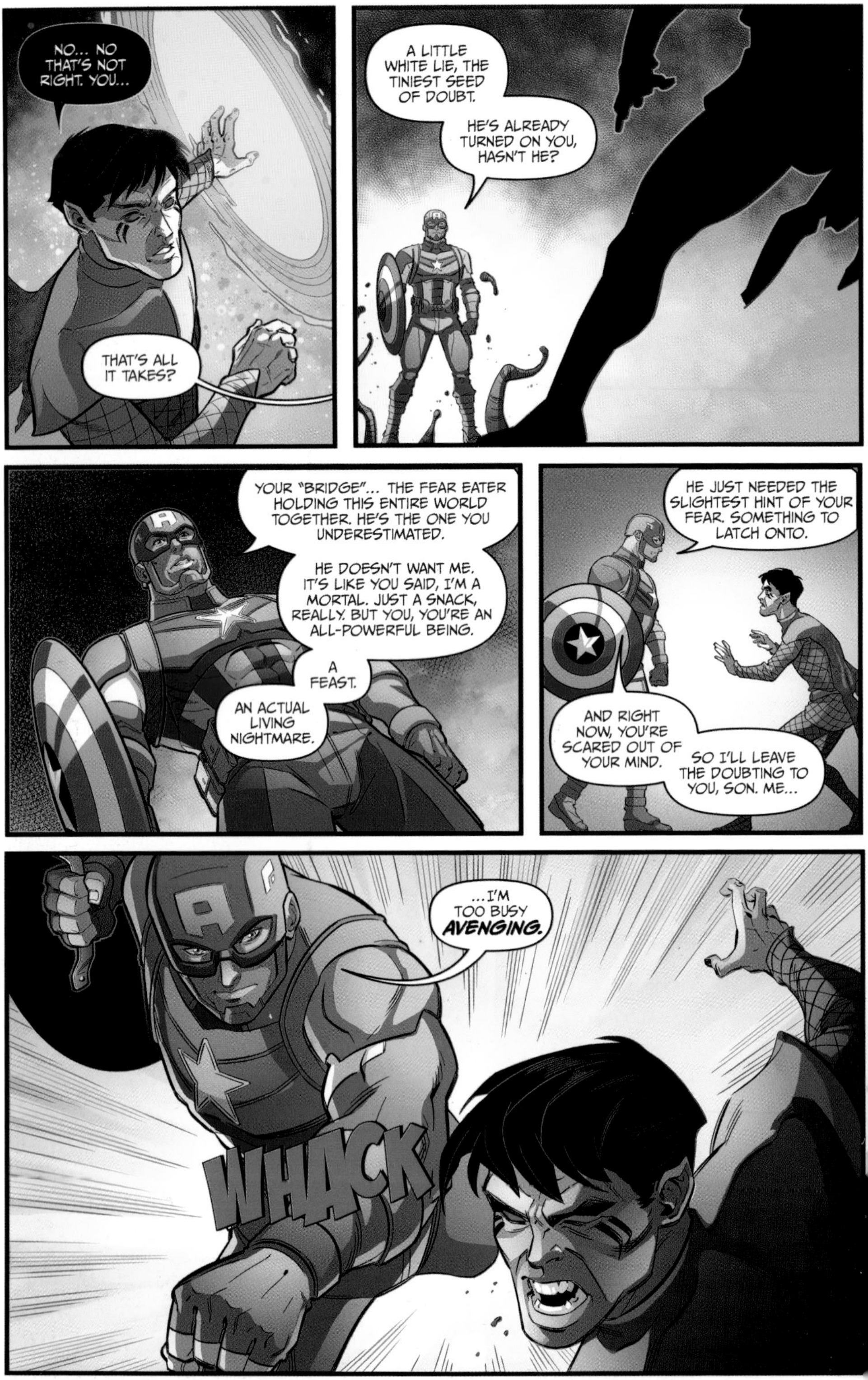
NO... NO THAT'S NOT RIGHT. YOU...
THAT'S ALL IT TAKES?
A LITTLE WHITE LIE, THE TINIEST SEED OF DOUBT.
HE'S ALREADY TURNED ON YOU, HASN'T HE?
YOUR "BRIDGE"... THE FEAR EATER HOLDING THIS ENTIRE WORLD TOGETHER. HE'S THE ONE YOU UNDERESTIMATED.
HE DOESN'T WANT ME. IT'S LIKE YOU SAID, I'M A MORTAL. JUST A SNACK, REALLY. BUT YOU, YOU'RE AN ALL-POWERFUL BEING.
A FEAST.
AN ACTUAL LIVING NIGHTMARE.
HE JUST NEEDED THE SLIGHTEST HINT OF YOUR FEAR. SOMETHING TO LATCH ONTO.
AND RIGHT NOW, YOU'RE SCARED OUT OF YOUR MIND.
SO I'LL LEAVE THE DOUBTING TO YOU, SON. ME...
...I'M TOO BUSY **AVENGING.**
WHACK

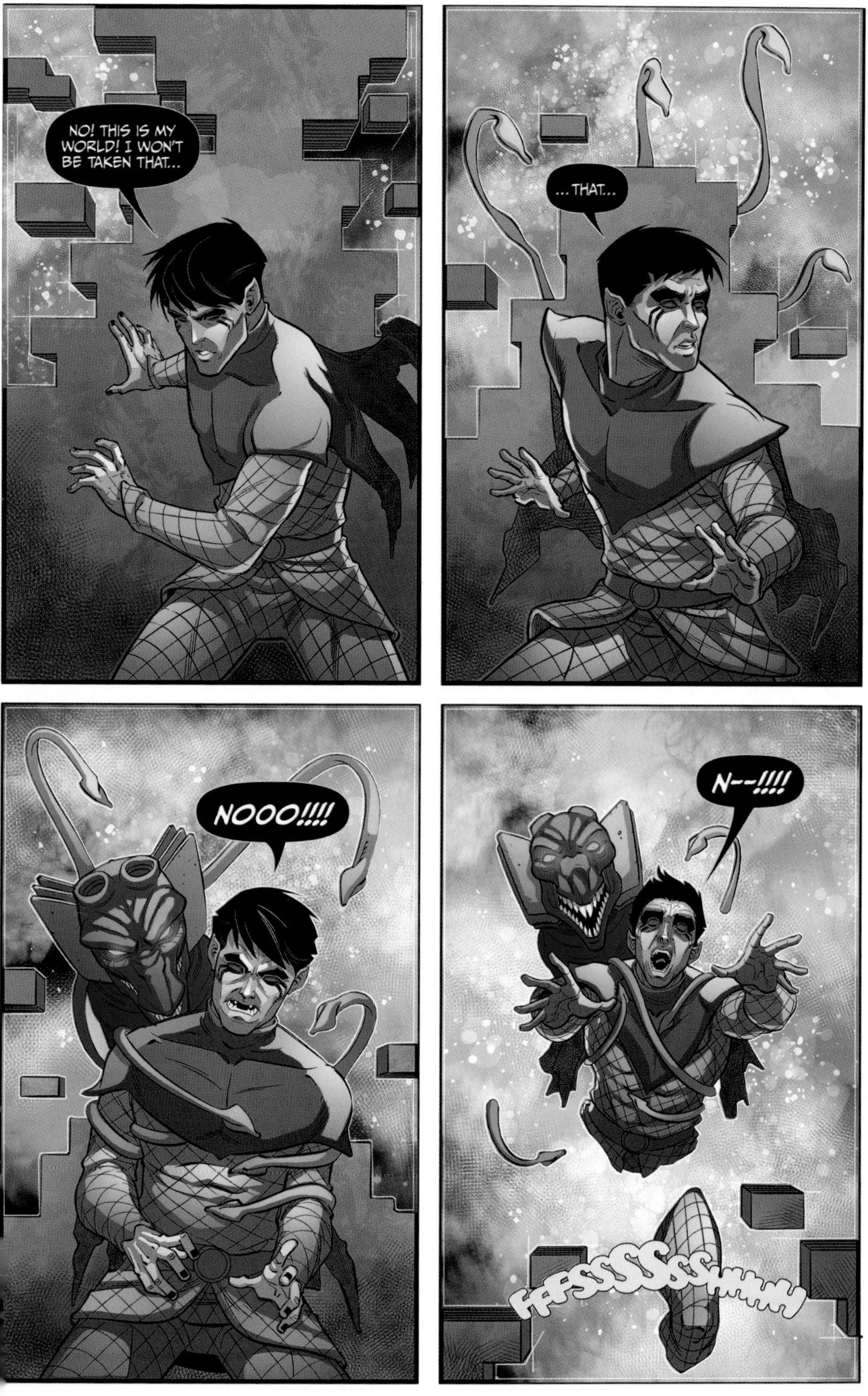
NO! THIS IS MY WORLD! I WON'T BE TAKEN THAT...
...THAT...
NOOO!!!!
N--!!!!
FFSSSSSSHHHH

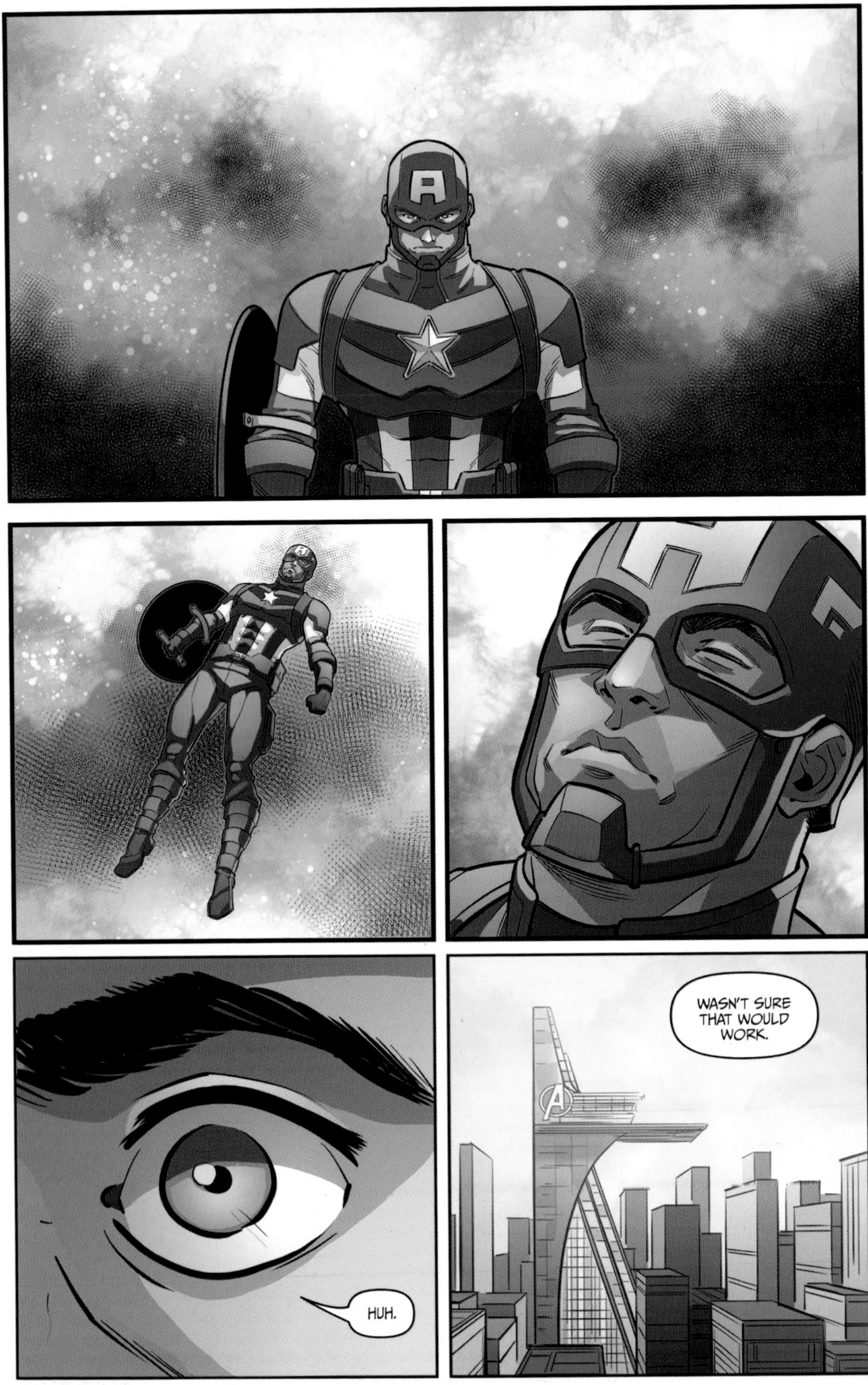
HUH.
WASN'T SURE THAT WOULD WORK.

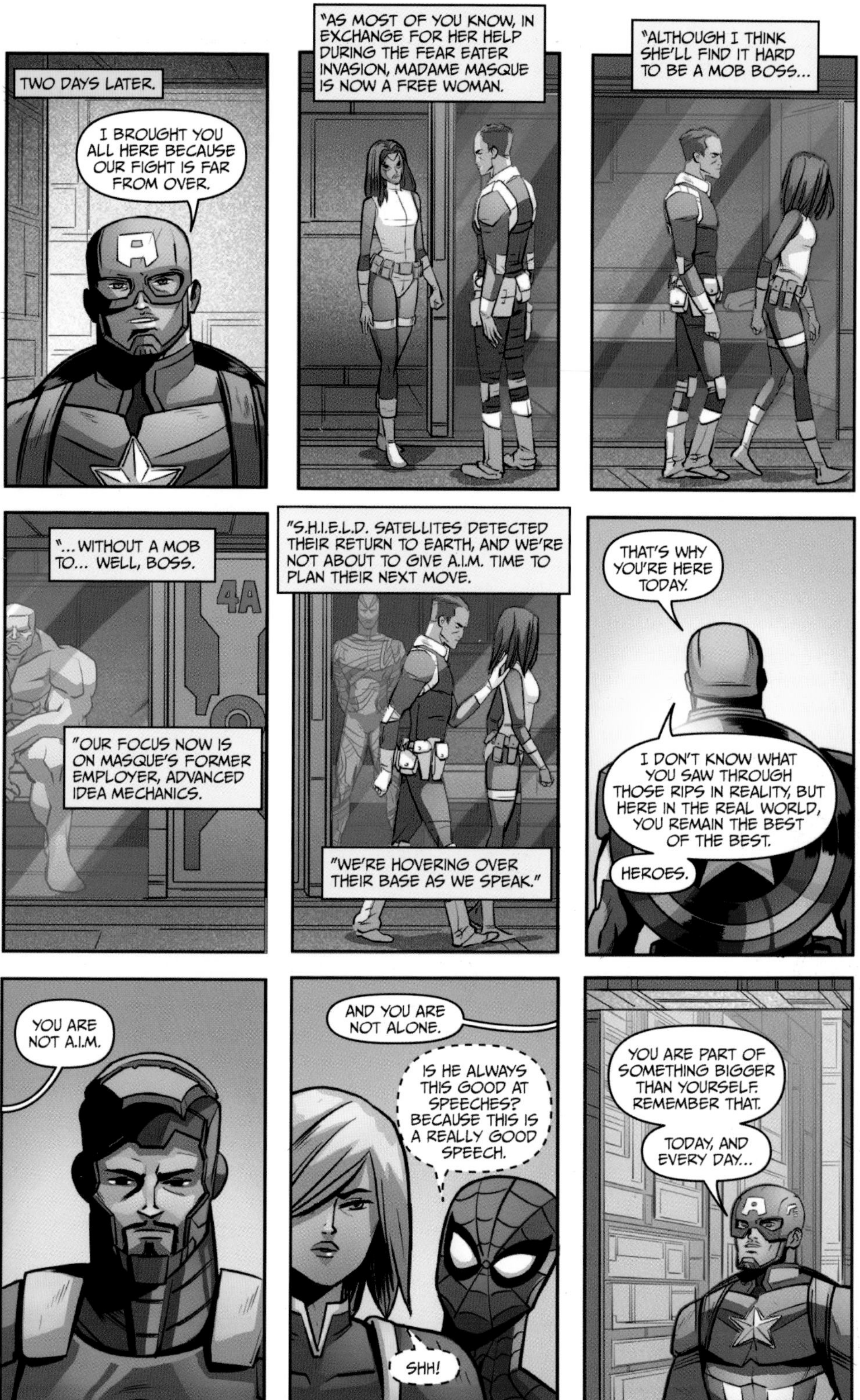
TWO DAYS LATER.
I BROUGHT YOU ALL HERE BECAUSE OUR FIGHT IS FAR FROM OVER.
"AS MOST OF YOU KNOW, IN EXCHANGE FOR HER HELP DURING THE FEAR EATER INVASION, MADAME MASQUE IS NOW A FREE WOMAN.
"ALTHOUGH I THINK SHE'LL FIND IT HARD TO BE A MOB BOSS...
"...WITHOUT A MOB TO... WELL, BOSS.
4A
"OUR FOCUS NOW IS ON MASQUE'S FORMER EMPLOYER, ADVANCED IDEA MECHANICS.
"S.H.I.E.L.D. SATELLITES DETECTED THEIR RETURN TO EARTH, AND WE'RE NOT ABOUT TO GIVE A.I.M. TIME TO PLAN THEIR NEXT MOVE.
"WE'RE HOVERING OVER THEIR BASE AS WE SPEAK."
THAT'S WHY YOU'RE HERE TODAY.
I DON'T KNOW WHAT YOU SAW THROUGH THOSE RIPS IN REALITY, BUT HERE IN THE REAL WORLD, YOU REMAIN THE BEST OF THE BEST.
HEROES.
YOU ARE NOT A.I.M.
AND YOU ARE NOT ALONE.
IS HE ALWAYS THIS GOOD AT SPEECHES? BECAUSE THIS IS A REALLY GOOD SPEECH.
SHH!
YOU ARE PART OF SOMETHING BIGGER THAN YOURSELF. REMEMBER THAT.
TODAY, AND EVERY DAY...

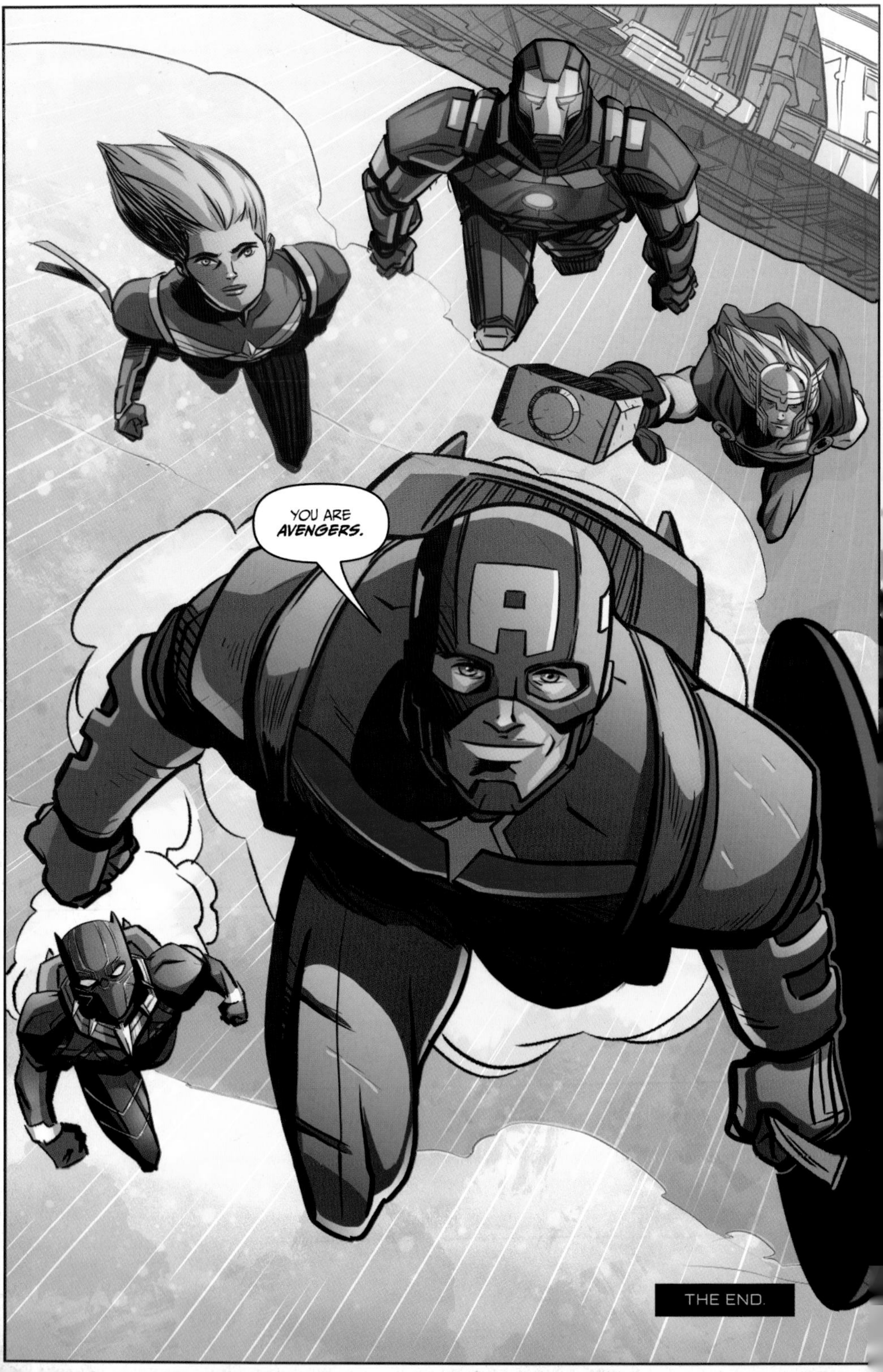
YOU ARE AVENGERS.
THE END.

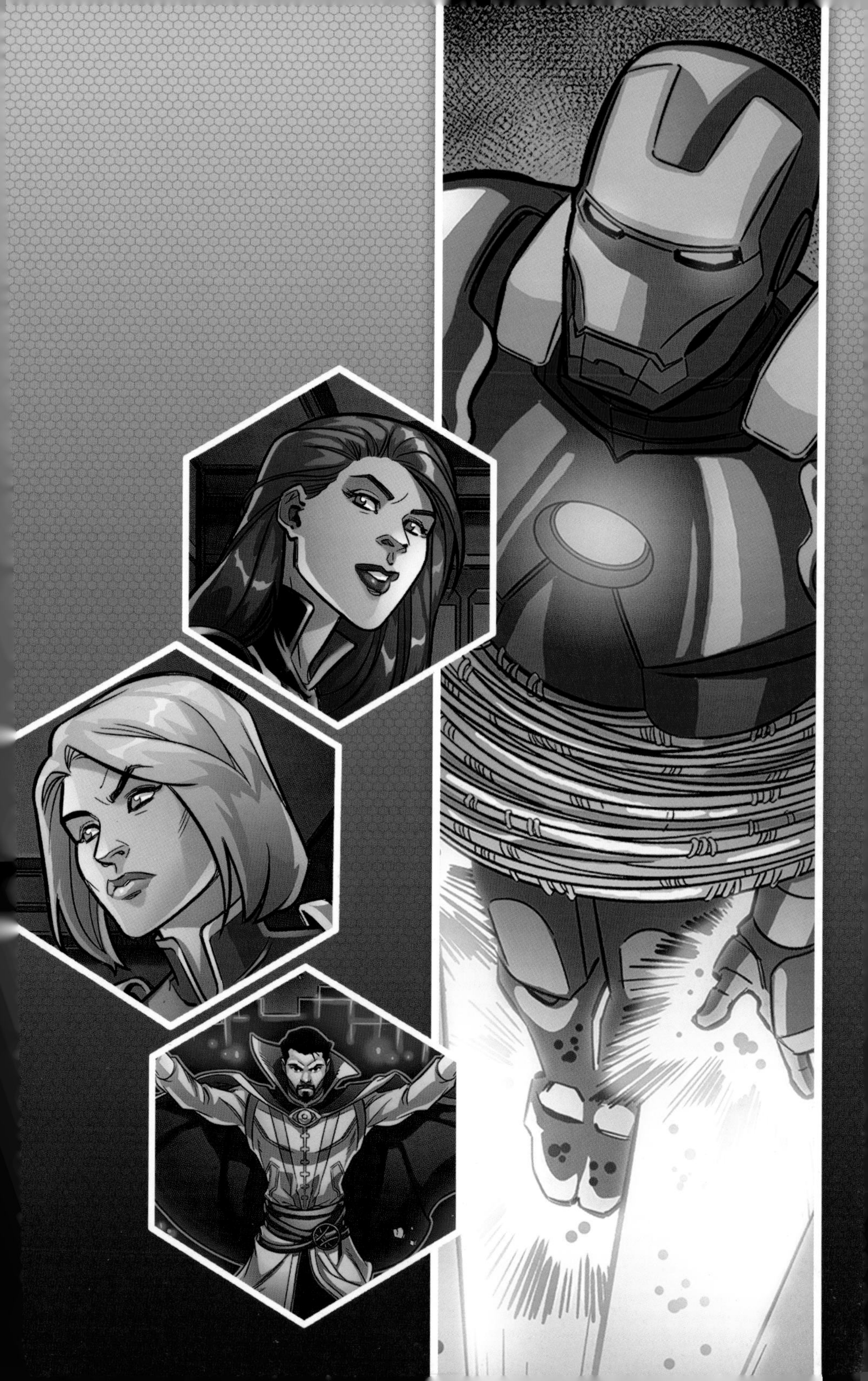

ART BY: LUCA CLARETTI

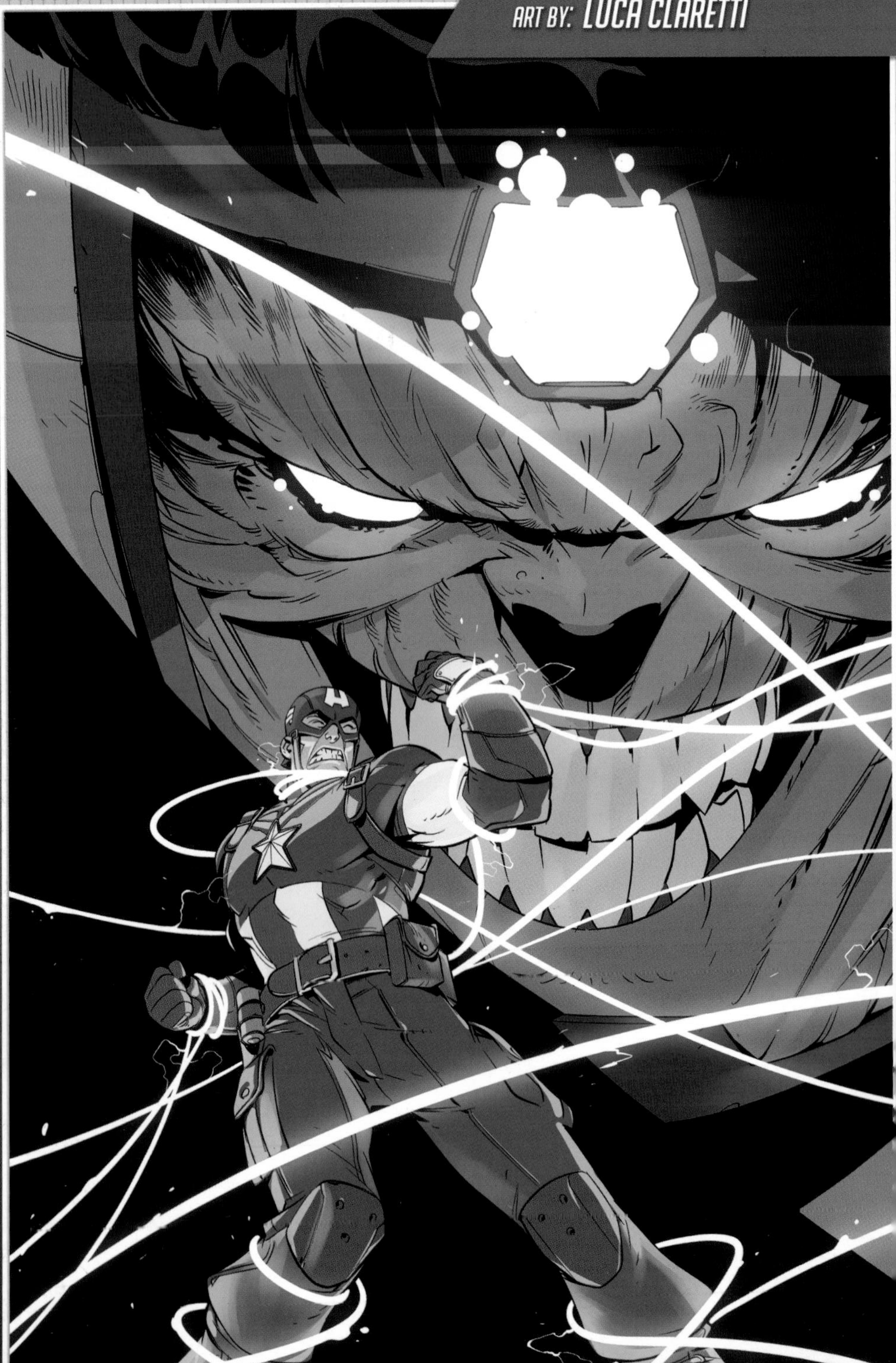

ART BY: NIL VENDRELL

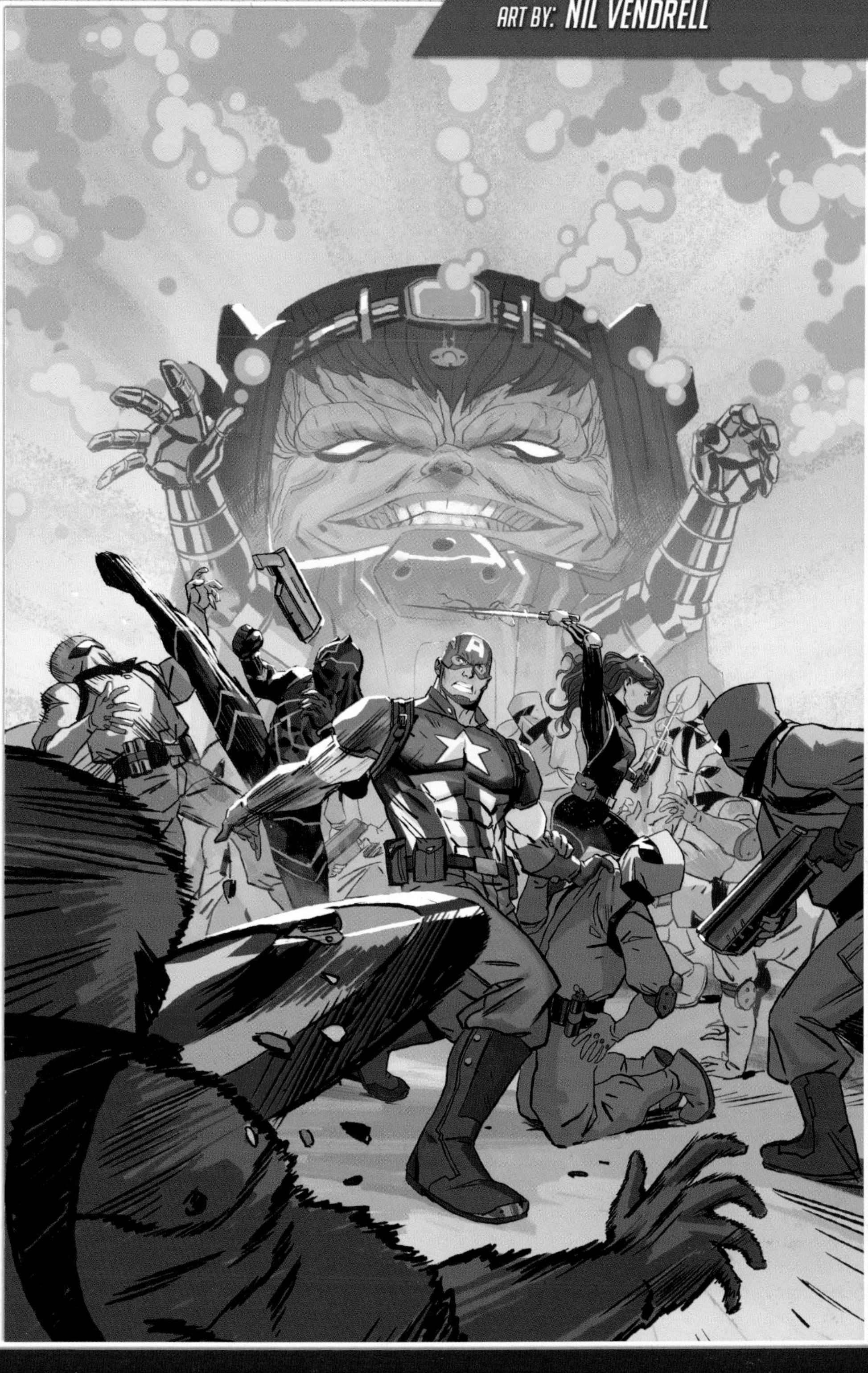

ART BY: EMMA VIECELI

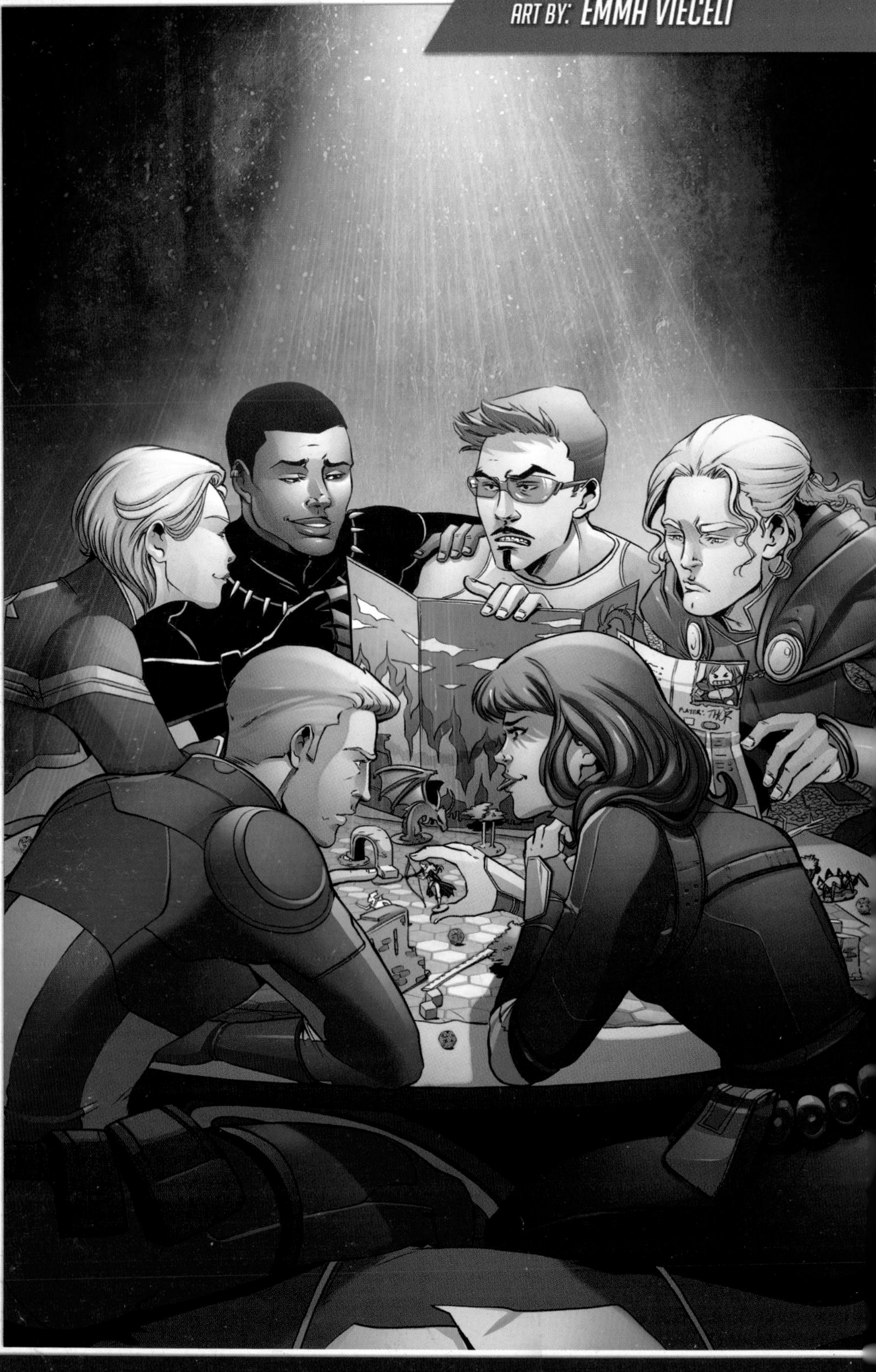
PLAYER: THOR